It's Crystal Clear
and
All about the Dad

Diane Brooks

PAGE PUBLISHING, INC.
Conneaut Lake, PA

First originally published by Page Publishing 2021

Please let it be known that most all the names, dates, and locations are fictitious as well as the medical and industrial techniques and awards.

ISBN 978-1-6624-6331-0 (pbk)
ISBN 978-1-6624-6332-7 (digital)

Printed in the United States of America

Lovely Rhonda, with her long wild rusty-colored hair, caught the attention of the man who would become her husband. They met in the most accidental way. He introduced himself in a most quizzical manner, almost as though he needed to think before he spoke. As the years went on, they had six children, and all their first names started with the same letter.

Not too long after, while still married to Rhonda, the same man meets a young flirtatious gal he can't get off his mind. She instantly speaks to his heart, and he loses it to her as well! Sweet Amy needs to ask his name at their second meeting, and again he answers coyly but with such feeling. They, too, are married and produce six children. Again, in this household, all the children's names start with the same letter.

Is this his scheme to remember who he is and who he was with and a way to remember his children's names? Who is this bastard? Just call him Dad.

It's really odd what can trigger the memories, but it happened again, as it has so many times over the years. Maybe it was the warmth of the late spring day or the way the apple blossoms filled the air with their fragrance. Maybe this time, it was just that Andrea needed the youthful feelings which were associated with the memories and the could-have-beens.

BOOK 1

Andi was a lovely girl of nearly eighteen with the world by the tail. Her senior year of high school was nearly over. She had a guy who could melt her heart and two tickets to the Beach Boy concert this Saturday night. Maybe there were concerts at the Worcester Auditorium before, maybe at other times with other performers, but that hadn't been in her realm of interest then. But now the sun rose and shone on Andi, her friends, and all that could be enjoyed by them. Saturday night couldn't come fast enough. First balcony, front row seats, and an extended curfew.

"Let me see the jumpsuit." The voice behind her nearly made Andi jump out of her skin. She didn't hear Lynn approaching by way of the orchard. The Chambers house was backed by an orchard as far as the eyes could see. It swung to the right side of their driveway, and a fenced cow pasture bordered their left-hand boundary, heading way downhill. The farm at the top of the hill made it a dead-end street. Lynn always used the path though the orchard to get to Andi's house. It was much faster than using the road, which was uphill from her house. Lynn knew her way around the inside of Andi's house as well as her own.

She used the back door, rushed through the laundry room to the kitchen up the back stairway, and bounded into Andi's room.

Once in, she closed the door and scooped up the garment and lifted it high above her head to see the full length of it.

"Oh! You are gonna love it. Mom and I went shopping for Abby's birthday present last night, and once I tried it on, both Mom and I thought it was marvelous." All of this being said while Andi shed her pants and top, kicked off her shoes, and took it from Lynn's approving eyes. She stepped into the front of a long yellow and turquoise one-piece outfit outlined in black paisley print, zippered at the front from top to bottom. Once zippered, she fixed a wide black belt with black chain link hooks around her waist. She did a model turn for Lynn to give her the whole picture. Squeals of joy and excitement escaped from both girls as they moved on to the subject of Andi's makeup and jewelry for the date.

Getting Andi dolled up for any occasion was really easy. She was a natural with thick, nearly straight, full-of-body dark brown hair with just the right amount of mahogany highlights to make it the envy of every senior in her class. Whether up in a do, ponytail, barrette, or headband, any way was always a good look for Andi. Her makeup was minimal as well. Why mess with perfection? But those eyes of dark green were to kill for, with the white flecks running through them, just like her mother's. And truth be told, just like her grandfather's as well (it was the tell of the Samson family). They were under perfectly shaped eyebrows that showed every expression she ever thought or felt, all surrounded by her flawless and naturally olive/tan skin.

Once back in her jeans that hugged every curve of her body, along with the ribbed green body shirt she'd tugged off earlier, Andi, with Lynn, headed to the commotion downstairs. Both girls, with their excitement peaked, headed for the kitchen where Abby was on the floor with assorted pots and pans while Andi's mom, with the phone propped to her ear, was busy making supper. Andi held one finger to her mom as she acknowledged the girls who came in the door as to say, "One more for supper." An affirmative nod from her mom was all they needed. Andi then dropped a kiss on her mom's cheek, and both girls headed out the door.

Lynn was always welcome to this already busy household. What's one more when six kids (minus Abby, of course. She's only just going to be two) are always bringing a friend or two home? Lynn and Andi had been friends since before first grade when Andi's family moved here from Norfolk, Virginia, near the Navy base. The family was considerably smaller then, as there was only her mom and dad, Andrea, and one older brother, Aaron.

Dad's job, attached to the Navy in some way, took him away often, but never long enough for the kids to cry themselves to sleep over it. When he got home, they were always full of questions like "Where were you? Do you sleep on a ship or in hammocks? Do you eat off tin plates? Or do you live normally in a hotel on dry land?"

His reply was always "I cannot discuss it. There is always a gag order on my assignments, but I am treated very well." The gag order comment always conjured up thoughts in Andi's head like torture and screaming and tears and things she saw in movies. The "I'm treated very well," added at the end of his sentence, took longer to wipe away than the other thoughts and sink in.

Her dad didn't talk about his assignments, the locations to which he traveled, or much about the people he encountered. But now and then, a name like Lieutenant Meyers or Fort Snelling or an order to be carried out would sneak out of his mouth. Most of these orders were crystal clear, not to be ignored or looked upon as requests. These orders generally took him away from home sooner than his week planned or his monthly four days earned at home.

Besides the fact that her dad would come and go, sometimes go before planned, life had been good to her mom and dad. Together, they worked very hard for all they had. A respectable six-room house to house four people twelve years ago was now a beautifully decorated twelve-room house that housed a family of eight. Amy used to tease that it was a good thing she had deep rich pockets, because every time Aspen came home, he was full and ready to spill. I didn't understand their private joke until Mom was pregnant with Abby. Now she knew what got spilled very time her dad got home meant!

With the addition of the twins, Alley and Alex, when Andi was six years old came major renovations to the modest little house. Dad, with his natural ability to picture the house he wanted, drew the plans, called the lumberyard two towns over, and engaged the CBs from a base in RI. And along with fantastic, knowledgeable neighbors, they had the roof off their house and a totally new five-bedroom, one-and-a-half bathroom top floor addition framed and completely enclosed over the long Fourth of July holiday. The bottom floor was yet to be roomed off, but her mom was unmovable in her belief that all bedrooms had to be on the same floor so she could hear her children. This was a fun time for Andi as she was allowed to stay with Lynn at her house for a few days while the construction was underway. The friendship between the two girls became a bond that would last a lifetime.

Today, as always, there was contentment for Andi's mom in this house. Her home, her family, her life was full of wonderment. Just the fact that Andi (and the other kids) enjoyed being here, bringing their friends here, entertaining here, sharing their lives with the others who lived here, pleased her mom beyond words. She listened to Andi and Lynn as they made their way upstairs, giggling over the plans they were making for Saturday night. Apparel was still the topic of conversation as their voices faded away.

Once back upstairs, Lynn once again was talking about the six kids, the always good mood of Andi's mom, and her easy way of figuring things out. Lynn was an only child, and her mom, albeit a very loving one, was always a wreck, making sure all things were always just right. Next, Lynn got on the very confusing subject of Andi's dad's compulsion with naming his kids all starting with the same alphabet letter. Andi's dad's first name was Aspen, beginning with an *A*. Andi's mom's name was Amy, again starting with an *A*. They figured it was a macho thing on her dad's part.

Then the mood changed, and Andi's voice became very serious. "Lynn, why do you have to go away to school? I'll miss you terribly. You're the sister I didn't have. If Aaron had been a girl, maybe he would have been my confidant, my sounding board, my shoulder to cry on and laugh with…but he wasn't. Since we were little, you have always been there for me. We were there for each other always. I don't think I like growing up. Too many things are going to change. I'm staying home and going to school locally. Summer is going to be too short!" Then the tears just started and wouldn't stop.

Lynn stepped a little closer to her, handed her a tissue, and told her, "Stop it. You're being silly, or way too serious, which is worse. Just think of the things we can do when we're older that we don't do now! Going away from home to school is a great idea. Monday through Friday, we'll be doing the same thing we are now. Just in different locations, but the weekends! Just think, you come and stay with me, *no* moms, *no* dads, just you, me, and a thousand other girls and boys."

"Stop it, Lynn. I am serious. It seems this weekend is just the beginning of the end. After Friday, we're out of school for a week. Saturday, we're all going to the concert. Sunday is Abby's birthday. Remember, Monday and Tuesday we're helping Mrs. Sargent with her spring cleaning. And do you know what Wednesday is?"

Puzzled, Lynn frowned and said blankly, "No."

"You're a great help. It's the lottery drawing of military numbers, you ninny."

"Depending upon the number Aaron's birthday falls on, he could be called to serve in the military. Since he is already in college, maybe he could apply for a college deferment. He should be okay. But Jake, he's all done school in a few months. If his birthday number is low, the military would take him in a heartbeat because he is not in college anymore. Besides, I don't care about the boys on your college campus. I care about Jake."

"You worry too much, Andi. Besides, I'm telling you, Jake is out for one thing, and it's not your good cooking. Look at yourself, girl. You're gorgeous. I've told you this before, so don't look so down. If his draft number is low and he goes, good riddance. Now how can we get a car to go shopping?"

Supper that evening, as always, was noisy. Aaron went to the community college in Worcester, lived at home, and drove in every day, so he was available to take Alex to this Little League practice, always with little Adam in tow. He was enrolled in T-ball that met only once a week, so Little League was a big thing to him. Alex was waiting with bated breath for Aaron to hurry up and finish so they could be out the door. Alley was going on and on about Spike at school beating her on the bike track again and it not being fair, and Abby was babbling between bites. She was so close to the table in her high chair that her kicking was rattling all the nearby water glasses. Andi and Lynn were between apprehension in asking for the car and exhilaration for the upcoming weekend. Mom and Dad were just there, listening and gloating over the activities of their family.

After the dishes were done and house settled into its evening hum, Andi approached her dad with cunning cuteness and wheedled the car keys right out of his pocket. "Thanks, and we won't be too long," she said, running out the door with her head turned back to throw her father a kiss.

It was nice to have her dad home again. It was always nice to have her dad home, but it wasn't often enough. If she looked at her mom's calendar, she'd see the pattern of every three weeks, her dad was home for four days. Three weeks later...four days home. It had been that way for years.

Family was very important to Andi. She loved the feeling of belonging and the love that was bestowed so freely from all her brothers and sisters. There was so much devotion in the family as her mom and dad believed in self-sacrifice in order for the kids to not go without or be left out of peer-related actives. The respect her mom and had had for every one of their children and the belief they had in themselves as trusting and honest people was a built-in lesson and way of life that Andi grew up with, lived with, and practiced with, not only her brothers and sisters but with every person she met. The trust which was bred out of these relationships carried over to Andi's now budding relationship with Jake, but the sense of security she had always known from love was absent with Jake, and she questioned the longevity of it if she didn't do what Jake wanted her to do. Could Lynn really know what she was headed for? Had the effects of a large loving family and growing up in a small town with basic religious beliefs sheltered Andi and wrapped her in a naive cocoon? Her thoughts were driving her crazy. She should trust Jake. He'd never given her any reason not to. It was Lynn and her endless chatter about his two-faced character. Andi had never seen it. Was it really there, just under the surface, and Andi didn't want to look that deep? Why was she feeling so...

"Yeah, Mom, come in," Andi said to a light tap on her bedroom door. Mrs. Amy Madeline Chambers was of medium height, medium weight, with short curly blond hair. The only thing not medium about Amy was her smile and infectious laughter. After six children, her hourglass figure was gone, but that did not distract from her natural beauty. There were no outstanding facial features, only the invisible angel wings and equally invisible halo which followed her everywhere she went. There wasn't a person who met her who didn't immediately like and respect her for her outstanding family and her outstanding work in the school and church. The hours in the day seemed to multiply when Amy had a chore to do or to finish. These chores or volunteer committee obligations were her lifeline to the community. But this visit to Andi was her needed lifeline to her oldest daughter. With Aspen away most of the time, she was both mom and dad to her children, but it was a life she loved.

"You and Lynn weren't gone very long tonight." It was just a simple statement that she knew would reward her with a response.

"Nah, we ran down to the mart for Lynn to pick up new underwear and a pair of shoes or sandals to wear with her miniskirt tomorrow night. She settled for swing-back sandals, but I could tell she's still not satisfied with them. Then I brought her home."

Amy picked up her daughter's brush and simply started brushing her hair like she did when Andi was just a little girl. There was comfort and tranquility as the older woman and the "becoming a woman" just sat in their own thoughts, taking in the surroundings of Andi's room. The net window wells that hung from side to side below the sills were still holding all of Andi's stuffed animals from yesteryear. The light turquoise wall paint Andi had picked out many years ago was barely visible beneath all her mementos. Shelves holding swimming trophies, pictures of many class trips and girlfriends, and of course, every popular rock band finished the ensemble.

At a change in Andi's posture, Amy looked at her daughter in the mirror as she brushed the shiny long dark chestnut-colored hair. Andi said in almost a whisper, "Mom, I'm afraid of the lottery draft numbers that are going to be picked next week. What if—"

But her mother cut in quickly, "Andi." It was an oddity. Her mom always called her Andrea. "Jake is a very nice boy who, in my opinion, is also very spoiled and accustomed to getting his own way. That, oftentimes, happens with the youngest in the family—heaven only knows, look at Abby—or an only child."

"But, Mom, what if he gets a low number and is drafted, can't go on to school, and I never see him again? And…" Andi's voice grew choppy and started to quiver.

Her mother broke in, "Honey, take it one day at a time. Wednesday is still four days from now. Don't ruin tomorrow night with these thoughts. You've been looking so forward to it. If by chance, on Wednesday, Jake's number is low, again live one day at a time and enjoy each other until he has to go."

"Mom, I've never felt like this about anyone before. The thought of him leaving…"

"Andi, you're a lovely young woman. You are going to love many times in your life. Each of those loves will bring a little pain. That's how you know it's real. It is how you handle those feelings and that hurt that builds your character and makes you the person you are or about to become. Your body is not quite finished growing yet, so don't stunt the growth of your character by becoming too dependent on one love just yet. There is a very special someone out there for you. Just when you think you're done growing, he'll be there. You will be ready for him, and then the two of you can grow together."

Their eyes met in the mirror, and Andi could see a dreamy look in her mother's eyes as she said, "Your father said he was born the day he met me."

"Mom, I love you, and I know you're right…but for the first time, I feel a tug inside. It's not that it hurts. It's…well…different."

With a gentle hug from behind, Amy smiled at her daughter in the mirror and backed out of the room, saying good night.

Andi's drawn face, which was looking back at her from the mirror, was not that of a happy-go-lucky girl about to go out on a date with a guy she was head over heels for, but at least her mother's words had given her an inner peace that lifted her spirits. Although she felt more at ease with her feelings, maybe, she was still torn between Jake's will and the respectable behavior which was expected of her. No, growing up was not at all what it was cracked up to be. She wished she could just wake up one morning an adult with all the in between nonsense over with.

Jake

At 6:00 p.m. sharp, Jake, along with Lynn and Tom, pulled up at Andi's house to be off for their long-awaited night out. As the three of them entered the house to say their hellos to the Chambers gang, Andi's dad motioned to Jake to join him in the garage for just a second.

"Hi, Abby," Lynn began as the little girl clung to her leg in a bear hug. "How's my munchkin?" she said as she picked up the baby and returned her affections.

Still carrying the baby, she lead Tom from the kitchen down the short hall to the family room, which was the last addition to the Chambers' house shortly after Abby was born.

"Hi, Ma" was the customary greeting Lynn bestowed on Andi's mom whenever she came in. Amy looked up from her magazine with a brilliant smile, and Lynn and Tom both could feel the love in the room.

"Hi yourself. You look great. Too nice to hide it away in a dark concert hall."

Lynn had always had a special place in Mom's heart as Andrea's best friend. She watched Lynn grow from that short skinny tomboy with a mouthful of braces into the lovely, curly, light-haired, still short beauty that stood before her today. Andrea and Lynn were opposites in all ways. Where Andrea was tall, Lynn was short. Andrea wore her hair long, and Lynn had short bouncy curls. Andrea was an introvert, where Lynn was an extrovert, and it showed in her choice of clothes for tonight. Her miniskirt was fire-engine red topped with a black nearly see-through short-sleeved lace blouse, a red ribbon tied around her neck, and long hoop earrings dancing around her curls when she walked.

Relieving Lynn of the bundle she was carrying, Amy said to Tom, "I bet you and Jake appreciate being out with two of Fisherville's beauties tonight."

With that, Tom watched Lynn, with a rakish grin, make her way for the back stairway to Andrea's room to hurry her along. Andi was just putting the finishing touches to her makeup, not that she needed any. Andi, with her long hair and matching long eyelashes that shielded the most vivid color of green eyes that sparkled with white woven into the green, needed no artificial powders to enhance her God-given high cheekbones, a strong slender nose, supple lips, and a perky chin. All of this was wrapped in a slight olive complexion (inherited from her mother's side of the family) without a flaw.

"Andi, come on…the guys are waiting." Lynn wailed when she rushed into Andi's room.

"Coming, coming. I'm about done. How do I look?" Andi said as she got up from her dressing mirror and pirouetted around for her friend to see.

Lynn's investigative eyes went right to Andi's feet. "I loved the wedges when you bought them, but I didn't realize they made you four inches taller. You go, girl!" Lynn exclaimed.

Andi's retort was "Don't bend over in that red thing."

What we had here was the classic naive and subdued personality paired with a devil-may-care personality, each, in her own right, keeping the other in tow. The differences in each girl's personalities was what made their friendship strong and never boring.

* * *

"Yes, sir, no problem, Captain Chambers. Tom just got the same spiel at Lynn's house. Mr. Marsden just reminded Tom of the one a.m. deadline too. Don't worry, we'll have the girls home on time."

After a handshake of understanding, Jake left Captain Chambers and went in search of the girls, all the while grinning through his teeth, wondering if the third degree from his adolescent girlfriend's father was worth the prize he was going to realize later tonight. *Tonight is the night*, he thought, his patience worn thin.

"Four months of polite conversation with these people, movies, dinners, bowling, long uneventful walks in the orchard, all to no avail. Money spent, time spent with her Goody Two-shoes friends, all to be paid off tonight. Her maidenhead, bought and paid for. Willing or not, she's mine...tonight. That military Chambers doesn't scare me. He's a dad like all others. Just talking the talk.'

Jake was still talking to himself and shaking his head as he went back toward the family room.

"Shake it off. Relax, you have this planned. Don't blow it now."

Jake took a deep breath, and he let his smile broaden as he joined the others. Lynn and Andi were mingling with the family and didn't see him enter. Immediately, his thoughts and feelings upon seeing Andi went right to loins. She was quite the prize, and he did plan on having her.

With another deep steadying breath, Jake said, "Everyone all set?"

Andi slipped her hand into his. "I am," she said, looking straight into his almost black, deep brown eyes.

"Okay, let's go," Tom said as he took Lynn's hand.

Andi released her gentle hold on Jake's hand and settled on the arm of her mother's chair. "Night, Mom. Tell ya all about it tomorrow." She dropped a kiss atop her mother's head.

As was planned that day, the four girls parked at the auditorium for five hours. They stood in line for the tickets to the concert. Everyone met in Auburn at the Flying Saucer for a junk food supper before heading into the city. The weather was perfect, just a slight breeze blowing, which seemed to still all of Andi's anxieties and dreadful thoughts from just a few hours ago. Then this little group mingled with the wild crowd at the auditorium.

Within minutes of finding their seats, the first act was announced. The first performers who had little notoriety, but in keeping with the times, wore tie-dyed bell-bottom pants and wholly T-shirts and beads, lots of beads. Granny glasses were covering their eyes only for effect as their vision was probably fine, and their hair hanging around their shoulders was their only claim to fame, as their music lacked what it took to move this audience to acceptance. After twenty-five minutes of unknown tunes and murdered popular songs was a ten-minute intermission. It gave the vendors little time to sell their overpriced T-shirts, posters, and magazines. The lights blinked several times to signify the real show was about to begin.

With the house lights near to off, the spotlight appeared center stage on drawn dark blue curtains. In an instant, singing "Surfin' USA" in their undeniable harmony, the Beach Boys appeared wearing blue and white striped shirts, khaki pants, and dad-approved haircuts. Their voices filled the hall, as did the cheers and whistles from the appreciable audience.

"These seats are fabulous," Lynn said as she leaned nearer Andi's ear. "I feel as though Brian Wilson can see right through me."

Andi merely nodded, never taking her eyes off the stage. After "In my Room," "Little Deuce Coupe," "Surfer Girl," "Catch a Wave," "Fun, Fun, Fun," their own popular songs, and a few anecdotes were all done with lights changing from blue to green to red to brilliant white, they did a medley of songs they announced they had written or cowritten but were made popular by other artists such as Jan and Dean and the Everly Bros.

The hall was filled with music and a capacity crowd of screaming enthusiastic fans. Worcester didn't host too many popular bands. Most of those went to Boston auditoriums and baseball fields, so it was no wonder that scanning the crowd, Andi saw many moms and dads judging for themselves this venue and its place in Worcester. The night was still cool outside as the Worcester residences went about their normal business. But inside the auditorium, it had heated up! Andi was lost in another world, one filled with excitement and glamour. This was her first concert, and she was enjoying herself immensely. After the second encore, the show was over. Hundreds of people were all heading for the exits, all recalling their favorite song or performer or just complimenting the entire concert.

Andi, holding tight to Jake's hand in order not to be lost in the crowd, was also talking endlessly about the performance. "Tom, who did you say was coming next month? I think I've been bitten by the concert bug."

Tom yelled back, "No concert, just the Harlem Globetrotters!" Andi was disappointed.

Checking the entertainment section of the paper for future coming attractions was definitely going to be in her daily routine from now on. This was a hit. Worcester would surely continue to bring in good popular bands and set up a concert schedule. She knew Tom Jones was coming, but she had no interest in that performer.

Even Jake had a wonderful time at the concert, whistling and hollering along with the others in appreciation of the music. But now as Andi was walking so close to him almost at his height due to her damn wedged four-inch soles, clutching his hand for security, he was wondering and scheming in his head how to turn this dependency into his own advantage.

For the most part, Jake thought he was not understood by nearly everyone who knew him. Not his mother, not his only cousin who he used to spend every summer with at the lake, and not the guys in school his own age. As Jake was a midlife crisis baby for his family and born to older parents, he gravitated toward older guys. He thought they were cool, so his thinking was older, his actions bolder, and his attitude toward things and people he wanted was unscrupulous. On the outside, his manners were impeccable, and his command of the English language was always used to his own advantage. Debating was his favorite pastime, and even when taking the devils' advocate stance, he would rein victorious in any debate. For this reason, he remained the captain of the debating team at school. Jake was just finishing his second year at Quinsigamond Community College, majoring in human development and psychology. All the knowledge he picked up here just went to feed his own ego and direct him in dangerous directions. The whys behind certain behavior patterns and the causes for these patterns were lost to him. His major concentration was the skill with which to mask these behaviors with acceptable social graces. He graduates with an associate's degree in two months. That's what made him eligible for the draft.

To his mother's delight, Jake's attitude toward what life had to offer rather than what life owed him took a turn for the better just before Christmas last year when he started seeing Andrea Chambers.

The change in him was immediately noticeable. Jake no longer chose to spend all of his time with the radical group he picked up with when he started college. Those people only seemed to feed his self-righteous attitude—attitudes which his mother didn't understand but saw grow stronger since the passing of his dad when he was a junior in high school.

Those were really hard times for Jake as his older brothers rallied to comfort their mom and make all the arrangements and see that the lifestyle which they had all become accustomed was not disheveled too much. His dad was a forty-year General Motors company executive. Therefore, he left his family well cared for financially with separate funds for each boy's continued education or head start in self independence. At that time, Jake was the only boy still living at home. Wayne, the oldest, was married with a family of his own. Harold was, although single, working and living in New York City. And Elliot was a junior executive at General Motors, a position his dad had groomed him for. Naturally, when their dad died, they all came home. For those two weeks, Jake felt like a stranger in his own home. Everyone treated him as though he were a fixture and talked at him rather than to him. Jake was not consulted on the major decisions, which were all being made, nor did he take part in the discussions which did, in fact, have to do with his future. In his mind, Jake had decided, *No more*. No longer would others take into their hands matters which were his to decide and try to mold his future. His already too mature and overbearing attitude was again going through some extreme changes.

After two weeks of hustle and bustle, they were all gone. His brothers, who he grew up loving and trying to imitate, and his older dad, too slow, too tired, and too old to be his buddy. Oh yeah, buddy to his brothers, coach for their Little League teams, Scoutmaster for Wayne, rowing coach for Harold in summer camp three years in a row, and cheering at Elliot's basketball games. But he was never interested or was too tired to attend any of Jake's school plays or debate tournaments.

Jake, at sixteen, was a very spoiled child. He drove the car of his choice, walked all over his mom, and mastered the art of academic excellence. Therefore, teachers and school personnel chose to ignore his all-for-me attitude. They saw him as a rich kid who, one day, would straighten out. Now, five years later, had he? His circle of friends were respectable, and his girlfriend was a sweetheart.

Okay, Jake thought. *It's 11:10 p.m., and we have until 1:00 a.m. If we can get out of this traffic and over to Joan's quickly, I'll have some time to work my charms and surely melt this ice princess.*

His thoughts were interrupted by Andi's tug on his arm.

"Hey, you're off in another world. Troy and Joan just had a great idea. What say we walk down to the ButterCup for some music and dancing? And that way, when we are ready to leave the city, there won't be as much traffic."

His back stiffened, but he replied, "Tonight's your night. If that's your pleasure, let's go for it." His heart certainly wasn't in it, but chalking up another brownie point was his current thought.

So all those who were eventually going to end up at Joan's for a midnight snack turned and walked down Main Street toward the ButterCup. The ButterCup was a teen club with live music, psychedelic lighting, popcorn, and no booze. Jake held his tongue as the other over twenty-one-year-olds in their group made no objections. To his delight, the club was mobbed and could not accommodate their party of fourteen. So the disappointed group headed back up the hill to their cars.

Picking up the pace, as it was now 11:30 p.m., Jake grabbed Andi's hand and pushed at Tom, saying, "Last one at Joan's is on the pickup committee. First one picks the music." And the little entourage all followed, running up the hill. With most of the concert crowd now gone, only the red streetlights slowed Jake's progress back toward Grafton.

Within seventeen minutes, Jake, Andi, Tom, and Lynn were the first back to Joan's house. The yard lights were on, and the garage was ready and waiting with a cooler full of soft drinks, a long table with covered platters of chips and dip, popcorn, cakes, cookies, fruits, breads, and a note that the meat and cheese platters were in the fridge in the corner. The note also read: "We should be home by 1:30 a.m. This area had better be cleaned by then and everything quiet. With that in mind…have a wonderful time, and we'll see you in the morning."

Andi and Lynn were the first to see the note, so they set about removing the covers from the food, making more room for the meat platters and sampling as they went along. In the meantime, Tom and Jake were stacking forty-fives on the stereo. By midnight, the party was underway with the seven couples eating, dancing, or just enjoying their first night of spring vacation.

After two dances with Andi, Jake's desires were again the foremost things on his mind. Holding her close, he could smell the delicate scent of her perfume and could feel the curves of her breasts as she pressed against him. With her arms wrapped around his neck, he had both of his hands to explore the back of her neck and the curve of her back. With each stroke of his hands down the length of her hair, he'd land just below her hips on the rounded portion of her buttocks. There, he would linger and caress and massage until he felt his welcome had lapsed. His hand then moved up her side, just brushing the sides of her breasts to her throat and up to her cheek and over to her ear. Two dances and he could take no more. As the song ended, he dropped a light kiss on Andi's temple and took her by the hand.

"Come on, let's walk" was all he could choke out.

Andi's head was also pretty much in a whirl. Jake's hands exploring up and down on her body had an awakening effect on all her senses. So as he led her out the side door of the garage, she just held on tight to his hand and followed.

Once outside, they hadn't walked too long when Jake turned and took Andi into his arms. He kissed her long and hard. Jake's strong arms held Andi to him in an embrace that softened once he realized Andi was returning his kisses and was arching her body to meet his. Andi clung to Jake, not wanting this moment to end. She had never known feelings such as these, and she was afraid to move, to break the spell. Jake, much more experienced, tenderly kissed Andi on her brow and her temple. He uttered her name as he nibbled briefly on her neck and then once again found her mouth. Very gently this time, their lips met. Jake's arms were still wound around Andi, and his hands were exploring once again the small of her back and the tilt of her shoulders. Her arms were up under his arms, her hands rubbing his back in the same rhythm with the gentle sway of their hips.

Andi, feeling warm and wonderful, felt the probing sensation of Jake's tongue on her lips. His mouth, now partly open, descended one again on her waiting, trembling lips. With great care and more patience then even he thought he had, Jake coached Andi through the art of tantalizing kissing. Andi learned that by using her own tongue, she could make the earth move and the sleeping birds sing.

Jake, too, could feel the earth move and decided to find a more secluded spot. Andi obediently followed Jake deeper into the backyard. The yard was skirted on two sides by woods and a fence on the third to ensure privacy from the neighbors. The tall bushes along the fence would also ensure the privacy Jake was looking for. Not a word was spoken between them as they were once again in each other's arms. First they were standing by the bushes, then sitting, then laying side by side in the cool grass. Andi broke away from the embrace and lay flat on her back.

"What a beautiful night," she said, looking up into the heavens. "That moon shines just for us." Her voice had a dreamlike quality.

Jake propped up on one elbow, bent over for another kiss. While they were so engaged in another probing kiss, Jake's other hand was very busy with the zipper that ran full length down the front of Andi's jumpsuit. After successfully unzipping three-quarters of the length of her outfit, he slipped his skillful hand gently under Andi's bra. In an instant, his fingers were fondling her perfect hard nipples. Andi's head and heart were in such a whirl that she never noticed his actions until his cool hand touched her very heated flesh. She put an abrupt stop to not only the kiss but also covered his hand with her own to stop him from fondling where she'd never been touched before.

Now with complete awareness and Lynn's words—"He's only out for one thing"—ringing in her ears, she spoke very slowing and clearly, "Please remove your hand. I'm not ready for what you have in mind."

With this, she helped him remove his hand and started to stand up. Infuriated with the coolness of her voice, Jake pushed her back to the ground.

With a touch of sarcasm and anger in his voice, he spat out, "What do you mean you're not ready? What in the hell has all this been to you? It's called foreplay, sweetie." His tone of voice softened, but his body language was full of heat. "And you play very well. Oh shit, Andi, I've wanted you since the first time I saw you."

Still, Andi said nothing, and there was a pause.

"I'm sorry I pushed…but you played like you were ready."

Now standing still without a word, Andi zipped her clothing back into place. Again, her head was spinning, this time with feelings of embarrassment and shame, but at the same time with feelings of exhilaration and somehow rather forlorn.

There was a long pause. "Jake, it's late. Please take me home."

Not wanting to discuss what just happened, Andi walked back to the garage. Once inside, her equilibrium returned almost back to normal, and she was able to say good night to her friends and hurry Lynn and Tom along. Lynn and Andi walked to Jake's car, but Jake wasn't there.

While Tom went to look for him, Lynn asked, "Where did you two disappear to, and what happened?"

"Oh, it's like you said. Jake was out for only one thing. He tried, I resisted, now it's time to go home."

"Just like that? Tell me what happened. What did he try? What did you do? Where were you guys? I looked for you. Damn, here they come. You better call me first thing tomorrow and fill me in on all the details."

Tom and Lynn settled in the back seat as Andi sat sidesaddle in the front in order to talk to Lynn, not even wanting to look at Jake. They had a conversation about Abby's birthday party tomorrow.

Jake sat, eyes straight ahead, and drove first to Lynn's house and around the corner to Tom's. They were alone again. Andi sat in silence until she couldn't take it anymore. In tears, she started to apologize. The drive to her house was only moments away. When they were in her driveway, she began, "I'm sorry if you think me a tease. I've never been kissed quite like that before, nor have I been made to feel like you made me feel. I'm just not ready to commit myself to anyone yet."

"I wasn't looking for a commitment...just a little relief. Relief from the tense physical position I was put into. I've wanted to touch you, feel you, have you for so long. Tonight was supposed to be the night. I thought all systems were a go."

"All the more reason for me not to permit myself to ever again be put in a position to have to say *no*. I never, ever want to be someone's relief. I had strong feelings for you. You've never voiced your feelings for me. You've admitted you wanted me, but that's only lust. I can't be just a conquest."

Jake said nothing to this but expelled a grunt of sexual disappointment. Still sitting and staring straight ahead, he began to adjust the sexual package in his pants, using the steering wheel as cover. Feeling a little more comfortable, he turned toward Andi and said, "It seems like I'm spending all my time with babies these days. No more. Get out."

She couldn't get out and away fast enough. But Jake also got out of the car. He followed her for only about three steps. He grabbed and held Andi by the upper arms and planted a kiss on her that curled her toes. It was the kind of kiss that she had to respond to. He felt this and was satisfied with her response.

"There, just a little something to remember me by when you are trying to sleep. You can also dream about what you are missing out on."

With that, Jake turned abruptly, got in his car, and drove away. Andi ran up the four steps to the breezeway and ran through the entry porch, not stopping until she was in the middle of the kitchen.

She heard the single gong of the grandfather's clock in the family room. In these familiar surroundings, she stood very still, trying to steady her breathing while wiping tears from her eyes. Then, while wandering aimlessly around, touching the backs of the chairs, rearranging the candles on the table, putting away the few cups and dishes on the side board, anything to keep moving, she reviewed in her mind the last five minutes with Jake and the whole evening with him.

Lynn was absolutely right, she thought. *He is out for only one thing. And, Mom, you're right too. I feel the fool. How could I have not seen it before now? He always wanted to be alone with me, yet he also conceded very graciously all the time to whatever I wanted to do. Mom said he was spoiled. That's not the behavior of a spoiled child. So was it a game to please me so I would please him? Well, it didn't work, so if it were a game, I guess I feel better and can consider myself the winner.*

With that, Andi went about shutting the lights as she made her way to her bedroom.

After leaving Andi, Jake drove down the hill and stopped at the end of the street near the orchard. He got out of his car and walked around in circles a minute, trying to clear his head. The ache in his loins and the letdown in his heart told him this was just another reminder that he wanted Andi to be more than just a conquest. Sure, he wanted to get laid, but what was it about this girl? Everyone said he was a nicer Jake since he took up with her. Even his mother liked him better since he was dating Andrea. With that, he wailed and punched a tree. Holding his aching, bleeding hand, he got back in his car.

Destination unknown, he just sped away. The first bar he passed was his present destination. He was alone and feeling quite angry at the world, and the beers went down so very easily. The dimly lit and very little place with its musty, stale smell was not what he wanted, so he moved on. The next bar and the one after that did nothing for his mood either, but still the beers were consumed one after the other. His barhopping had taken him out of town, and it had grown late, so he headed back toward Grafton. He was very tipsy now, which did nothing to smooth his foul mood. He went straight back up the hill toward Andi's house, cursing all the way.

"I could have had that blond two bars ago or the one at the bar I just left, but I don't want them. Andi, what have you done to me? Okay, I'm here...now what?" he murmured to himself.

He parked his car just before her driveway in the shadows of the apple trees, quite unseen. After walking around noiselessly for what seemed like hours, trying to formulate a plan, he walked up the front steps to the house and tried the door. To his surprise, it was ajar just a bit, and he entered the house without any problem. His eyes already adjusted to the darkness, and his knowledge of the house allowed him to proceed directly to the staircase that went up the stairs toward Andi's bedroom.

If only he hadn't been drinking. If only he had been more observant while outside the house. If only he hadn't been so hell-bent on the one conclusion to this night. If only he had smelled the smoke when he did enter the house…if…if…if…how different everyone's lives would have been!

Jake's senses were not up to par and not working properly due to all the drinking. All his thoughts and efforts were still in only one part of his body, and that had steered him to where he was now. But now…three sheets to the wind, he vomited and retched dry heaves, standing in the front hall of Andi's house. He panicked, cried, and fled as fast as he could. He got in his car and raced down the hill.

At the very same moment, with Jake soiling the front doorway, there was another man making his way up the back staircase to Andi's room.

Double Exposure

Fisherville housed something very unique for a small township—a large factory, one that bused employees in on a daily basis from Worcester and bus stops along the way. New people walking around Fisherville and Sandersville Monday through Friday, during the day, was not an odd occurrence. Because of this factory, there were more coffee shops and sandwich shops and diners along Main Street. These little shops were kept busy Monday through Friday by the people that were always bused home after their work shift.

Some of the new people working at the factory worked smart and saved their money. They bought a car, stayed in town after work, and frequented the local restaurants. After all, this was how a small town grew.

Working in a factory, for some young men, was just a financial stepping-stone to something better. Learn the neighborhood and surrounding towns. Meet the young women who work in the stores and restaurants. Investigate higher education in this location. Feel out the surroundings for better jobs and housing. That was the goal for many men in many rural towns, but not for these two. They were on a mission. One was out for revenge, and one was a tagalong for excitement. They were a pair to beat a full house, and they were out to prove it.

Rockwell, age twenty-two, second oldest son of Rhonda and Reginald, resided in Towson, Maryland, with his five other siblings. Rockwell was six-foot-one with curly black hair always worn short because of the curls and wide shoulders thinning down to a narrow waist. He had long skinny legs and thick glasses. He was waiting for the day to get corrective surgery to shuck the glasses and become a most handsome him…more like his older brother Russell, always the stud and never the student. For him, it was money for college. Not contact lenses or corrective surgery, just college. Rockwell was always doing this or that for someone else, always the pleaser, as his mom would say. He was a good kid, attentive son, great older brother, and excellent student. He just graduated college, four years at Rensselaer Polytechnic Institute, or RPI in Troy, New York, pulling a 4.0 for the last three years. He was always the student, never the stud! He lived in an apartment on Tenth Street just outside Washington Park. He shared this apartment with Kevin, who also just graduated from RPI.

Rockwell was always doing, so he could live up to what he thought his dad would want or appreciate or honor for him to become or be, but never quite reaching that proverbial excellence. Well, things have changed…changed in a big way since he saw the manila envelope in his dad's trunk on the floor. He prayed his mom didn't know the contents of the envelope and vowed to keep it that way. So why did he (his dad) have such a damning piece of evidence in this house, in an unlocked box in the trunk that was always locked? Rockwell had many times tried to snoop in his dad's trunk when he was away, but it was always locked. What a big mistake he made this day walking away from it unlocked.

The pictures! Dad lied again. They did come back. He just didn't want us to see them. One by one, Rockwell looked, no, examined each picture. They were all together, those he took and those Russell took. They brought back such fun memories. Except looking at them now gave him a stomachache. *What was he looking for? What had we captured that he didn't want us to broadcast?*

The new clothes…no, Mom knew about that…staying in motels… we talked about that a lot, so it can't be that. The crazy bitch, shaking her boobs all over the place and coaxing Russell away with beer. Mom wouldn't be too happy about that…but those are vacation memories, nothing to get you panties in knots about!

Hey, what's this? I never saw this in our motel room, hotel room either. They are our rooms. That's my hat on the table next to the TV. Double exposure…I wish it were clearer. Here it is again…double exposure. I wonder what we were really trying to take a picture of. Looks like the same note, just used and reused. I guess Russell wanted to ask him about it when we got the pictures back. If Mom saw it, she'd probably want to know how many times he left us alone while he went out for a drink.

"I loved those hot dogs." Rockwell caught himself saying that out loud! That apple orchard, that house, even the hot dog stand… he knew where he was. He knew he'd been there before!

There she is again! Wait, now he was on a mission.

Still sitting on the floor at his father's trunk, forgetting about the time, he looked carefully at each picture, trying to pick out the prints with *her* in them. Once he starting looking, she became more familiar. There were so many. Now he tried to put them in order by the vacation spot, by the background or other people in the shot.

"At ten years old, I don't know if I would have scrutinized the pictures in the same way…but I can see why he didn't give them to us. He's more than a bastard," Rockwell muttered. "I wonder if she is the one who lives in the house on top of the hill…above the orchard in Fisherville. Is that her gorgeous daughter in those other pictures? He's such a fool to first be messing around on Mom…but second to have pictures of her and her family here in our home.

"I just remember a wonderful vacation with my dad and my older brother. Why couldn't it have stayed just that! It's my fault for snooping. All those times I wanted him…*no,* needed him home when Kevin was hurt or when we were in the hospital together. I've got to stop thinking!

"Damn…he used us to be with her! The notes on the TV…he was sneaking out to be with her!

"Thanks for the graduation present. I knew you were a blowhard, knew you couldn't possibly fill the shoes you were always so proud of. I'll find out…they were probably bought with lies too! Thanks for the gift. In my knowing, it's not just me you've lied to and cheated out of a half of life! You weren't even a part-time dad! I liked my life a lot better at school. I counted on me and only me.

"Why did I snoop? Because *I am* his son!"

So this day, Rockwell shoved the envelope in his pants, ran from the room, and started to formulate a plan. He'd prove that he could make a plan, execute it, and excel. He needed to do this, lay it at his father's feet, and watch his house of cards collapse and burn. But before that, the missing envelope would burn a hole in Daddy Reginald's heart and brain. Rockwell was only sorry he knew his dad's secret. It blew his world apart.

Kevin Schaffer, Rockwell's best friend since first grade, also grew up in Towson, Maryland. With backyard games, cartoons, broken leg from falling out of a tree, board game champion, and the beginning diagnosis of his bone cancer, sixth grade was epic for both boys. As it turned out, Rockwell was the bone marrow donor who saved Kevin's life. Life goes on. Kevin, now six-foot-four, had full body shoulder-length dark brown hair, always clean and shiny and pulled back with a short length of rope. He had the hair girls would die for or just like to run their fingers through.

Kevin's mouth, with supple full lips, was always smiling below twinkling eyes women got lost in. His long straight nose was centered between high cheekbones which gave him a masculine appeal. To say he was handsome was an understatement, and he knew it! But Kevin had a problem. He didn't deny himself any of the sensual or causal pleasures his looks or money afforded him. Rockwell was always picking up after him, and Kevin used that situation.

Over the years, the association between the two boys became almost toxic. Rockwell excelled in academics and his chosen field of synthetic fuels, and he helped Kevin hide his almost insatiable sexual appetite. The appetite, fueled by his good looks and booze, was used to mask any of his inhibitions.

They always backed each other up in any situation, and so far, life was good. It was an easy friendship Rockwell and Kevin shared.

With graduation over, all the thank you notes written (because both moms said they had to), and life becoming too homey for them, Towson held very little interest for either one of them. Rockwell was getting antsy to implement his plan and wanted to move on. Leaving his mom and the kids was just like returning to school. As usual, his dad was not at home...always away for his job, but was he?

They were two clean-cut young educated males on the prowl with prospects for new jobs in a new city. Kevin was just along for the adventure when Rockwell announced he was headed out of town to begin a new life in a new town.

What the heck, he thought. New horizons meant new conquests. He'd give it a try. A few months somewhere else was as good, if not better, than staying here. "But Fisherville, where the hell was Fisherville? What's in Fisherville?"

By way of very little explanation, Rockwell promised Kevin would encounter at least one very attractive female.

The road trip was pretty uneventful. The weather cooperated and they had normal traffic all the way north into a corner of New York on I-95 just like they were going back to school.

"All highways look alike," commented Kevin.

"We've made this trip so many times in the last four years. The highways have become familiar. That makes it an easier trip," countered Rockwell.

But the trip was a little different. They didn't continue on I-95 but headed to I-84 in Connecticut.

"Kevin, check the map. How far away are we from Massachusetts? Can you see Worcester on the map? That is the biggest city near Grafton. Can you see Grafton on that map?"

Kevin unfolded the map and studied it for just a minute. "Yup, straight ahead for nearly sixty more miles, then we merge onto the Mass Pike. That will bring us through Springfield and another forty or so miles to Worcester. Need exit number 11 into Grafton. You didn't tell me we were going to ride forever without a burger and a beer. Stop, man…stop!" he strongly suggested.

It was maybe when they got off the highway and stopped for that burger and a beer that Rockwell got quiet and thoughtful about having Kevin along for his dirty deed. He was also thinking about the Mass Pike, a toll road. He would get a ticket to get on and pay to get off. It hadn't been built yet, but he knew he'd been to Grafton.

Little town after little town, he and Russell counted how many school buildings, churches, and police stations were in those little towns, one after another. No highway back. That's how they came upon a movie house in one of those small towns. It was a great show. The memories were killing him!

Then and there, he filled Kevin in on his intentions. By tomorrow, they'd be on the road again. "So, Kevin, pick a place, open the map, and point. By my calculations, we will be back on the road by three a.m."

Kevin was dumbfounded, first by the information and second by what Rockwell intended to do. This wasn't Kevin's first rodeo for dropping into a town, getting plastered, chasing, exploiting as much pussy as time allowed, then heading out of town before the sun came up. So he'd do it again! But for Rockwell to have such evil thoughts and deeds to accomplish was so out of the ordinary.

Grafton was a quaint little town. The grass was greener, and the sky seemed a little bluer than it was at home or even in school. New England, yes, pretty as a picture. That was something he'd heard before. *Strange memories, strange thoughts, shake it off.*

It was Kevin's shiny black 1963 Chevrolet Impala SS Two Door Hardtop 327 V-8 named Betsy that they drove into Grafton. Once here, they almost enjoyed driving around the picturesque little town. It didn't take too many miles or too many turns for them to find Speer Street. They went up the hill, following the orchard. (He had seen pictures of this orchard, the one he and his dad and his brother played in that summer. *Shake it off.*) They went all the way to the house at the top of hill. Rockwell slowed considerably to get a better look at the house and maybe people in the yard. All quiet. No people, no dogs to bark. They were in luck. Rockwell pulled to the side of the road. He reached for and opened a bag from the back seat that had pictures in it. Same cow fence, the same driveway heading to a house that was very different. It had gotten a major addition built on, same garage, no doubt the same family living there. Same name on the mailbox—Chambers.

If more had changed, maybe fate would have steered Rockwell in a different direction, but some things didn't change. A lying, cheating, dirty bastard of a father deserved what was coming his way!

The road went no further. It was a dead end with a farm at the top. They had turned around and were heading back down the hill when a car drove into the Chambers driveway. They slowed just enough to watch a very beautiful young woman get out of the car. She bent to retrieve something from the front seat, showing panties while doing so. She was talking to an equally good-looking woman behind the wheel of the car. The younger woman—girl, really—backed out then straightened and made her way up to the back door.

"Who…is…that? She's gorgeous!" Kevin exclaimed.

"I told you you'd meet a very good-looking girl here in Fisherville," Rockwell muttered.

"You know her? Do I get a meet and greet? When?"

Rockwell stepped on the gas again because Kevin was nearly out the door.

They drove back down the hill and around Grafton for a short time until they stopped at a Howard Johnson's in the center of town. They learned a lot from local residences having lunch, always spouting their local gossip. For instance, the goings-on tonight for the teens was the Beach Boy concert in Worcester.

"Maryanne, did you see the short one that's always hanging around that pretty Chambers girl in Lenners on Tuesday? I'm shocked her mother is letting her wear that outfit out of the house, never mind to the concert."

"So we have a very short window in order to conduct our business tonight," Rockwell said. "At about midnight or one a.m., when the girl gets home, you make your move. The beauty you saw at the house is the only female this town has to offer you, pal, so you make your move on her. I know you can be stealthy when you need to be, so have fun with her! I'll be in my spot taking care of my business and ready to leave this town behind by three, just like I said."

"When and how do we meet back up?" Kevin asked while drinking his third beer, getting a start on tonight's inebriation. Kevin's drinking was the reason Rockwell did most of the driving.

"Remember the orchard we passed going up the hill to the girl's house? I saw an access entry road near the beginning of the orchard. I'll meet you there at three a.m. sharp. If I'm not there, get out of town…fast. I'll meet you at the apartment at school on Wednesday."

Needing to pass more time before tonight's exploits, Rockwell drove around town, just making his heart sick at seeing more of the sights he had seen twelve years ago while being a passenger in his father's car. He saw the factory his father told them about, the hot dog shack where they ate foot long dogs, and the park nearly across the street from the hot dog shack where they were stopping now just to stretch their legs.

The Deed

Kevin made himself comfortable behind the fence in the orchard, which was behind the garage in the Chambers' backyard. It was early, so to keep himself occupied and busy, he brought along two six-packs of GIQs to help him wait for the tall sexy girl to arrive home. Time either drags when you're waiting for an ultimate dreamed-up sexual pleasure or flies by with the help of many beers and sweet thoughts. So it was either a long time before he heard the car pull into the driveway or just a short time. He wasn't sure. He also wasn't sure it was Rockwell he saw prowling around the garage just a few minutes ago...was it just minutes?

But he listened to every angry word uttered between the two people who just arrived home from spending the evening together.

"Get out!" he heard the young man yell...then not much more after that. Just a few minutes later, the back porch lights went out, the car drove away, and everything was quiet again.

"Okay, showtime. Let me show that little flirt what her date couldn't accomplish. Poor him. My turn to party."

So with that thought, Kevin started making his way to the back door, the one Andi went through just a short time ago. Once in, he needed to let his eyes adjust to different levels of darkness, and then he proceeded through the mudroom into the laundry room, past the washer and dryer toward what looked like the kitchen. But he encountered a stairway on the left, so he went up. He was standing very still to make sure no one stirred. He tried the first door. Nope, two boys. The next door, two girls. Across the hall…bingo…the sweet smell of female.

Entering the room, Kevin nearly tripped on clothes or bedding or whatever was on the floor at the foot of her bed. He bent over and picked up a pillowcase and quietly made it to the head of the bed.

The adrenaline that was pumping though his body as the thoughts of imminent success were racing though his mind and his loins allowed him to slip the pillowcase over Andi's head and just about get it tied with her robe belt before she awoke, screaming. He let just one scream escape from her before he slugged her upside the head. Standing alongside Andi's bed, looking down at her unmoving form, Kevin waited to see if her scream had awakened anyone in the house. Half scared out of his mind at being discovered, he stood unmoving for several minutes in the darkness of her room, listening to the quiet sounds all around him. With his courage up to continue his quest, he lifted his prize and was stepping out of her room when the clock in the family room started it's gonging of two in the morning. Not wanting to be found with Andi in his arms, her head covered in bed linen, he rushed down the hall and out of the house. He froze again, listening to the still quiet all around him and realized the only sound he heard was the mad beating of his heart. With his heart beating so rapidly and his libido building to near explosion, he still didn't smell any smoke.

It was a very short walk to the car, and when he started stuffing Andi in the back seat, he noticed, for the first time, that she was wearing a short nightdress of the sheerest material. Her legs were warm where they rested on his arms, and her breasts rose and feel with the rhythm of her breathing, Her nipples rubbed against the sheer material, but her breasts slipped out of the material as he bent her body to fit her into the car.

One mouthful of those delicious little nubs now will hold me until I get her down the hill, he thought, so he proceeded to nibble and caress until he needed to fix his position in his pants, before he could straighten up.

Once behind the wheel, Kevin headed back down the hill, took a right into the orchard, and drove in ways not to be seen from the road. This wasn't a very heavily traveled area with mostly residences. Once parked, he retrieved a blanket from the trunk along with a piece of rope. With the blanket spread on the ground, he proceeded to strip naked, rub his six-pack, chest, flat stomach, and grope his long, thick, throbbing manhood.

Grabbing the other blanket from the trunk, he went to get Andi out of the back seat. He wrapped her cooling body in the blanket, sat on the other blanket with her head in his lap, and hyperventilated while touching the lace that laid upon her perfect body. Once he had his breathing under control, he fondled her breast and caressed her nipples. He rubbed her smooth arms and tongued his way over her firm flat stomach and on down to the brown triage between her legs.

The still of the night with the sounds of the spring peepers and the breeze rustling thought the trees, mingled with the faint sent of Andi's perfume and the steadiness of her breathing, helped to calm Kevin's nerves, but not his longings. In what seemed like hours, Andi finally started to stir when Kevin's fingers, or was it his tongue, aroused her never before touched sex lips.

Now, quite comfortable playing with Andi's sex toys, Kevin didn't notice her movement toward her head covering, but her scream definitely got his attention. Now he was snatching at her hands to get them away from her head, and he rolled her over to tie them behind her back. He said in an almost inaudible voice, "Stop struggling. It will hurt a lot less that way."

"What do you want with me? Who are you?" she spat out as quickly as her mind would allow. "Where are we? Who are you?" she repeated again.

Kevin made no attempt to answer her questions but spoke in his controlled masculine voice, "Shut up and do what I tell ya." He dropped his head to her left breast and suckled nosily while his hands were kneading and pinching at the right breast.

Andi's legs were kicking and striking out in all directions while she continued to scream.

"We can't have this behavior now, princess. I am going to be real good to you. Make you feel things you'll like that you've never felt before and give you plenty to think about this whole time." Kevin covered her entire body with his, letting his penis slide down between her legs and just press there while he tried to control himself.

She was frightened beyond words. Andi's whole body began to shake as she remembered something foreign being tied over her head and then being hit in the head. That's when everything went black. Now, feeling things she'd never felt before but not being able to see who was touching her, she began to shake again.

Once Kevin had his erection under control and could function with it in his way, he moved off Andi, rolled her over again, shackled her legs together with his hands and arms, and went down to her vagina and began sucking and stretching flesh in his mouth.

He was caught in his own sexual frenzy. Her screams and coughing and gagging were just part of the night noise. Kevin continued to use and abuse the warm body beneath him, tugging at each nipple with clamped teeth while jamming one then two then three figures into the hot center of Andi's sex box. He continued his assault on her body until there was no more noise. Andi's body had just gone limp…not fighting anymore, not kicking anymore.

Making sure Andi was still breathing, Kevin was thinking, *Okay, baby, you just make this easy for me.*

With very little control left, Kevin positioned Andi on her back, legs spread just enough to give him entry to her sexual center. Between her legs, Kevin began to make his entry toward that center and lost control and rammed into her. That action brought Andi back to screaming and rolling and fighting once more. That action was also all it took for Kevin to lose control, and he was easily spent.

"Damn, that was quick. Now I can take my time while taking you the next time," he whispered in her ear as he continued to slide in and out, working himself into another frenzy while getting as hard as a rock, never giving her a chance to relax.

"That's more like it, baby. Make it hard. Make it good. Good girl, play nice. I don't like it easy." All while Kevin was talking to Andi, he was pumping at her, biting her neck, pulling at her breasts, and generally ripping her apart. "I've heard virgins don't like to play rough. I guess I had to find out for myself. You're good, sweetie. You know just when to submit, go limp, and be quiet. But when you fight back, that rage really sends me! Rockwell's gonna hear about you. He'll be pleased that we took something of you just like your mother took something of his father. Rockwell was so angry when he saw the pictures. I wish I could take a picture of you to share with him. Show him how much fun I had and how much I enjoyed you. Then we could send it to both of them and taunt them secretly. This is revenge for Rockwell."

His first strike into her hot center accomplished, Kevin changed positions. While leaning up on an elbow, he continued his assault, letting his cock slide back into the throbbing cavern. He started rocking then rocking harder and still harder until once again, Andi's psyche couldn't handle the abuse, and she passed out. With her still body, Kevin loosened the tie around her neck, found her mouth, and let his tongue roam around in that hot moist little pocket to his heart's content, while still continuing his sliding in and out, kneading one breast and then the other.

This was the part Kevin liked the best. His cock took on a life of its own, knowing its own rhythm and timing. It allowed his hands and fingers and mouth to conduct their own exploration of the rest of her body. Without even withdrawing out of her now slippery little snatch, he repositioned himself, first to retie her head covering and then to bend her leg to a position where he was able to suck on her toes and rub her behind the knees. With all extremities busy in one spot or another, Kevin became quite comfortable. He was letting all of his bodily movements function without thought or reason. It just felt good. It made him feel good. She still wasn't moving. No reason for him to do so either.

"Thanks, Rockwell. She's a dream. I only needed this one girl in this town. She was worth waiting for. I wish we had a picture of this for that bag of yours."

Relaxed as he was just now, with the girl laying straight out, him still cradled tight in her vagina, his hands, fingers, mouth, and tongue exploring and touching and smelling and tasting the sweet aroma of female, he still hadn't smelled the smoke. Then all hell broke loose. Fire alarms filled the quiet around him. Andi's body jumped, and that reactivated Kevin's penis in a big way. He immediately started pumping and sliding in and out and ramming at her with such force, she could only cry and endure. His large hands held her to him with such force, he was afraid he might have broken something…an arm, a rib. But then he relaxed his frenzy a bit and spoke soothing words of enjoyment and fun and next times, and he gently brought his orgasm to its finality, speaking more words of appreciation and giving her an A plus for her cooperation. He could tell…she passed out again!

Now gripped with fatigue from sexual release, Kevin rolled away from Andi to his back and just lay there, taking long hard breaths. Wanting to sleep but uncomfortable with a cold wet penis exposed to the air, he turned, slid his not quite ready member back into the wet and waiting vagina, and willed it to work. So back and forth, in and out, once again using hip action, he relaxed with his penis locked inside Andi and slept.

With a startled jolt, he slipped out of Andi, sat, and needed to reacquaint his memory with his location. Once he felt a little more composed and aware of his surroundings, he smelled smoke in the air. Looking skyward, he noticed the night sky light up with flames reaching high into the clear night. Now he remembered…the sirens of just a few minutes ago. He hoped it was just a few minutes ago. All at once, becoming aware that he was in a very dangerous position, Kevin pushed Andi aside with a "Thanks, babe" and ran to the car. He grabbed for his clothes, dressed in a hurry, threw one of the blankets in the back seat of his car, started the engine, and said, "Okay, Betsy, get me out of here." And he drove to the edge of the orchard and back to the road.

Just as he approached the road, it became busy with police, fire trucks, ambulances, and recuse vehicles. He couldn't pull onto the roadway, and there were too many apple trees on either side of him to turn around. He backed up a bit and sat and waited. He was feeling just a little anxious of the package he left not thirty feet behind him, and knowing he could go back to her for round two, he did the next best thing. He pushed the car seat back, released his pulsating penis from its binding, and began to enjoy himself, thinking of the tight little pussy he just conquered. Then he jerked off. This helped him to relax as the traffic proceeded up the hill.

Realizations

As with the beginning of any beautiful morning, the first thing Andi always noticed were the birds singing and the sunlight streaming through her bedroom window. But this wasn't the beginning of a typical morning. Her whole body hurt in places she didn't know she had places. Her neck hurt from something tied around it. She opened her eyes and saw drab colors of blue and rose and turquoise. Her head hurt terribly. Her hands were still tied behind her. She dug her nails into earth...dirt. Now she had the sensation of being cold, very cold, and wet. Having no comprehension of her situation, no memory of the events that put her here, no sense of direction or ability to move, sheer terror ebbed into her every pore. Screaming hurt her throat. Tears and sobbing shook her to exhaustion, and she blacked out, which was a saving mechanism.

At four forty on the morning of April 12, 1964, the Fisherville Fire Department responded to a call at 17 Speer Street. Being it was a structure fire with possible injuries, neighboring towns were called in for support. It was a big fire, a disastrous fire fueled by forty-five-miles-an-hour wind blasts with a promise of a storm brewing but not arriving. The fire consumed every floor and every corner of the house. Two cars in the driveway sent the message that all occupants should be home. Those two cars were also lost to the fire.

Many residences of Speer Street started lining the road and watching in sheer horror as the fire grew and was blown to every untouched corner of the house. There was a fireball in the night sky, and smoke filled the air on the entire hill. There was nothing anyone could do. The fire department was working tirelessly to extinguish the flames, but they just kept reaching for the sky and spitting fireflies into the night. The wind fueled the flames, and there wasn't enough water at the top of the hill to fight the flames.

Lynn heard the town's fire siren wailing for many minutes before seeing many fire trucks proceed up Speer Street. Now quite awake, smelling the smoke, hearing the commotion, she dressed quickly and also headed out and started following a fire truck up the street. On her heels were her folks, who were also at the ready and needed to see what was going on. By 5:00 a.m., Lynn, Carol, and Jeff Marsden were joined by a dozen or more neighbors just watching the Chambers' house get destroyed by fire. Lynn ran off by herself in search of someone in charge to inquire about the family. She was looking for Andi. She ran from one cop to another to an ambulance person to anyone that would talk to her. No one knew anything about the people in the house. No one could get close to the house. It was just too hot and too dangerous a situation. Too many people were too busy to talk to her. With all the people and commotion and noise and danger with sunrise just about to happen, Lynn's world was closing in on her. She felt helpless and worried sick, but she was easily walked home by her mom because her dad promised to stay on the scene for any information.

Once home, Carol Marsden's mothering instincts kicked in, and she provided hot tea, a sleeping pill, and a blanket wrapped around Lynn's shoulders by her own worried, loving arms.

Once entry into what was left of the house could be attained, the chief needed a head count immediately as he knew there should be eight people to be accounted for in the home. At 11:14 a.m., there had been seven bodies carried out of what was now just burnt hopes and dreams and smoldering embers. The frantic search in the shell of the house and around the yard for one more family member turned up the eighth body, several feet into the garage area, burnt beyond recognition.

To most people in town, it was just another beautiful spring day. Many knew that there had been a fire at the top of Speer Street, above the orchard. They all hoped the orchard had not been touched by the fire. Again, many were curious about the house fire, the people in the house, and the orchard. Many of those people set out for a walk to quench their curiosity.

Dan and Helen were longtime dwellers of lower Speer Street and knew everyone that built on or bought property going up the hill. Dan was even an extra hand when Aspen and company put the addition on the house. Nice people, he remembered. Their walk started in the orchard going toward the water tower, the source of most of the water for Fisherville residences if they didn't have a well, over to the blueberry bushes, then up further into the orchard.

The farther up they walked, the more pungent the air got from smoke. This started to fill them with dread as to what they would see once they reached the residence, but they continued. Helen took the lead, crossing the beaten path cars made to enter the orchard. She stopped suddenly when she saw an unusual looking pile of dirty clothes…no, a pile of rags…no…

"Dan, quick, look at that lump of colors down there. I think they moved."

Dan and Helen ran to the spot where they saw a young woman on the ground in a fetal position, naked, covered in blood and dirt with her head wrapped in what looked like a pillow slip. Shocked at her appearance and the fact she was not moving, neither Dan nor Helen wanted to go near her.

"Stay with her, Helen. I'll get help." Dan was not a young man, but he moved as fast as he could back toward home to call the police. But as luck would have it, once he stepped out onto to Speer Street, a police car was coming down the hill. Dan flagged him down, shouting and waving until the cop pulled over. Once Officer James Stricker heard Dan's breathless explanation of his dilemma, they rode together in the cruiser back into the orchard to the girl in trouble.

Immediately, Officer Stricker radioed for an ambulance, opened his trunk, retrieved a blanket, and carefully approached the young woman on the ground. With a calm and soft voice, he started to explain that he was merely going to cover her cold uncovered body and try to uncover her face. Even at his words and his gentle touch, there was no movement from the girl. Within minutes, the ambulance arrived.

"What the hell...now what?" said Brad Willis to his partner, Kelly Mint.

"Same street, same day. What mean guy took a bastard pill?" was Kelly's response. But Kelly didn't waste any time untying the knot that was around Andi's throat while Brad was attempting to take Andrea's vitals. Attempting, because Andi fought against him touching her. She screamed and wouldn't listen to any of the soothing words being spoken to her. She kicked and wiggled and cried and passed out again. Kelly finally got the cloth off Andi's head to expose a bloody mess of a bruise on the side of Andi's head. Helen was watching as the girl's features revealed who she was. Dan had to steady his wife as they realized it was Andrea Chambers.

Everyone in the orchard at that moment needed to take a second breath, because not thirty minutes ago, the local news announced that, and naming them by name, all eight family members were lost in the fire. Kelly stayed with Andi and held her hand all the way to the hospital. She was very careful not to let anyone see the tears that escaped down her cheeks.

Once the ambulance had safely deposited Andi at the hospital, curious onlookers all wanted a chance to talk with her. Not today. They weren't going to. She was barely conscious. Every time a person went near her, Andi would retreat like a wounded animal and faint into a safe slumber. Her unconsciousness made it easier to examine her and record the brutality she had lived through. They found bruises on her face, cuts around her lips, left ear torn from pulling on earrings, scratches down her neck, purple welts on her breasts, nipples nearly ripped off, bruising and tears to her vagina, thighs, and ankles with bite marks.

These were physical horrors. She still had the nightmare of losing her family to live through.

The next hour was a blur to Andi. Nurses were washing her, dressing her into a hospital johnny, wrapping her in blankets, and were forever taking her temperature. She didn't want to think, so she let them do as they liked. She was x-rayed and got stitches in her left ear and more on the top of her head. She didn't want to think, so she let them do as they liked until now. Another doctor wanted to examine her in another unfamiliar manner.

With the verdict in on Andi's condition and the discussion with the police, because there was no sign of smoke inhalation or no odor of smoke on her person at all, the team that examined Andi believed she was taken by force from her home before the fire started and raped.

Lynn had been awakened by the phone ringing, and at the same time, her dad, Jeff Marsden, came into her room to wake her. It was around one in the afternoon, and she had been in bed long enough. Her head was still in a daze, and she needed to be spoken to about the events of the day. In the meantime, Lynn's mom was in the front yard with a policeman getting what facts he could disclose regarding the fire at the house and Andrea's condition.

"What do you mean Andrea's condition?" Carol blurted out. "That was a cruel thing to say. She's dead." With that, she was in no mood to answer her ringing phone.

With a sincere apology, Officer Striker asked Carol to sit down and talk with him for a minute. Carol's posture was stiff and deliberate in showing the officer to a living room chair. Just at that moment, Lynn and her dad entered the living room with curious looks on their faces. Why were the police here? They also took a chair.

"Okay, we are sitting now. What is this about, and why are you here?"

"I believe that phone call that just went unanswered," Officer Striker began, "was from the hospital to request you go there for a very important meeting regarding the Chambers children. Particularly Andrea. They were also requesting this immediately and offering everyone a ride to the hospital to facilitate the meetings and disclosures as soon as possible."

"Meetings with who and information about what and why Andi in particular? I don't understand. At least fill us in. You are talking without giving us any information." Carol's voice was a whisper carried on a sob.

"I'm sorry. I have no information beyond the request to transport you to the hospital as soon as possible, in that you were the closest people to the Chambers and Lynn, Andrea's best friend."

Jeff Marsden announced that he would drive to the hospital and try to lend whatever emotional support he could muster. The family members somberly grabbed jackets and car keys and walked to their car. Officer Stricker led the way with blue lights on all the way into Worcester.

"Okay, we are on our way in," reported Stricker over the radio. "The Marsdens are very confused and know nothing of Andrea's ordeal. They still think she perished in the fire."

Lynn was Carol and Jeff Marsden's only child. They had wanted more children, but it didn't work out for them. So they embraced the relationship they had with the Chambers. When Andi started coming around, she generally had one or two or even three extra kids tallying behind. Lynn became their second big sister, and Carol Marsden loved the noise and the activity of the house when they were all there. Cookies, crumbs, crayons, and mud pies were all the reminders of family life, even if most of that family wasn't hers. Now that was gone in an instant, and she felt such pain. Life was just not fair.

The three of them drove to the hospital, which was about twenty minutes away. There was total silence. Upon their arrival, Mr. Marsden parked the car in a designated VIP area as pointed to by Officer Stricker, and they all started to walk in together.

Lynn was determined to speak to someone in charge and get some answers as to why they were summoned like this. So in they walked. For Lynn, it was more like a march through what felt like a tan tunnel with dim lighting with dark blue lines on the floor. The lines were the direction to the emergency unit where they were sure someone would know the name Chambers and would be able to help them. But before they could even go through the glass swinging doors, a nurse appeared and suggested they follow her. She began talking to ease their minds, trying to assure them that once they met with Dr. Harkness, there wouldn't be such a mystery to unravel. Little did she know, this was just the beginning.

Lynn and her folks were led to a small room with about fifteen straight-backed black vinyl chairs. The radio was set to a channel with soft elevator music meaning to sooth, but who were they kidding! Lynn was fidgety, Mrs. Marsden wiped tears from her eyes frequently, and Mr. Marsden was thinking, realistically, how much help could they be?

In the meantime, Dr. Harkness was located and thrilled to hear Andrea's only "friends of record" were here for her. He knew first he would need to talk with them, determine their closeness with the Chambers family and Andrea, and fill them in on Andrea's condition and future shock. The next few hours were not going to be easy ones.

Dr. Harkness asked that the Marsdens be shown the way to his office on the third floor. Their wait hadn't been too long, and each one of them thought how serious a situation all this really was. After the introductions, Dr. Harkness got down to brass tax. "Lynn, I pray you are a strong young woman, because Ms. Andrea Chambers survived, or rather, escaped the fire at her home last night and is going to need every bit of your strength."

There was a long pause and looks of confusion and lack of understanding. Finally, Jeff Marsden, made his way over to this daughter, laying his hands on her shoulders. He asked the doctor, shaking his head, "You said Andi is alive?"

Now he really needed to hold Lynn down. Carol also reached over to take Lynn's hands. She was wringing her fingers together, looking at each of her family members with tears in her eyes. She simply asked Dr. Harkness, "Is Andi here now? Was she hurt terribly bad? Can we see her now? How did she get here? Was she burned bad in the fire? Does she know about her folks and all the kids? We thought all the Chamberses died last night. There were eight bodies…" These question trailed off into silence as the news of Andi being alive started to sink in. The doctor let Lynn rattle on. He saw her trying to shake her nervousness.

"Andrea has not been told about the fire or her parents or her siblings' deaths. Her injuries are not fire related. We believe Andrea left the house before the fire. There is no sign of smoke in her lungs or injuries related to that tragedy."

At this, Lynn was jumping out of her chair. "I need to see her… where is she? She would never have left her house last night. She'll tell me what happened."

Lynn was settled back in her chair by her father to hear more of what Dr. Harkness had to say.

"I'd hate like hell for her to get the ugly information about her family from an uncaring source or the press. So for now, we just would like you to be with Andrea, be her friend, and be evasive about any facts as you know them because I'm afraid hatred will become an anchor if the facts are not disclosed in a proper manner. Just in the last few hours, she has been asking for her mom and has been subject to hysterics when she isn't getting any answers to her questions."

Dr. Harkness rubbed his face from exhaustion once he stopped talking.

Carol Marsden understood fully that he was asking Lynn to be Andrea's strength when she was told the truth about her family and when they started asking her questions about her ordeal of the night before.

Dr. Harkness wasted no time and continued, "This is how the police and the hospital want it handled. There has been a crime committed against this family, so we want to move quickly and quietly. Lynn, this is where you come in. I'd like to schedule an appointment with Dr. Gayle, a psychiatrist. Dr. Gayle Hampshire and myself want to meet with Andrea, with you by her side for support, to tell her about her family. Do you think you can handle that?"

She knew she could not answer that question. The lump in her throat was quite evident. He continued, looking directly at Mr. and Mrs. Marsden, "Mr. and Mrs. Marsden, Lynn, I haven't addressed Andrea's injuries suffered upon her body last night because the how and who hasn't been answered yet. That leads us to the second crime committed last night. That information to be told to her is also very painful information. She was found, naked and bound in the orchard close to her house, having been brutally raped."

A knock sounded on the office door, and Dr. Harkness allowed entry to Officer James Stricker, investigating the attack upon Andi's body, and Officer Oscar Pooler, investigating the house fire. Lynn, trying to take all of this in yet ignoring the names and their responsibilities, only wanted to see Andi.

Impatient now, she blurted out, "Take me to Andi now. I need to see her." Carol took her hand in a calming manner, looked at the doctor, and nodded agreement.

Now that they were there, standing, peeking in, Lynn saw Andi's face and started to cry. Andi, sensing being stared at, looked up and saw her best friend in the whole world approaching her in slow motion, and all Andi wanted to do was hide and make the room and all the people in it go away. She didn't want Lynn near her to smell the dirt and shame that she was sure was radiating off her skin. She didn't want her shame to color their friendship or change the way they felt about one another. She wanted yesterday back with her mom fussing in the kitchen and the kids filling the room with their noise. For Andi, that reality was gone, and she didn't even know it yet.

"Hey, girlfriend…" She couldn't even get the whole word out. She just approached Andrea with open arms. She landed on the bed and wrapped her arms around her friend like a wet blanket.

Many minutes and lots of tears later, from both girls, the hug ended with Andrea's sobbing voice. "I'm so sorry. Please don't hate me. Get off me, I hurt there."

Lynn jumped off the bed, took a good look at Andrea's face, and held back more tears. There was no more time just now as Dr. Harkness came in with a little cup of pills with an order for Andrea to down them with a sip of water. Once that was accomplished, Lynn and Andrea sat holding hands. Dr. Harkness said the pills were a mild sedative and should work fast, given Andrea's state of mind. She needed to sleep—a deep healing sleep that would help her absorb all the devastating facts that were going to laid upon her, he hoped.

Carol stood in the door way, thinking, *They don't need me yet. Lynn will do just fine. God help Andrea.*

Lynn noticed Andi's hands starting to slacken and loosen their grip on hers. Dr. Harkness returned with a list of items he wanted to review with her. First, he noticed that Andrea's breathing had slowed to a more normal rate, and she had indeed fallen asleep. "She is definitely going to need this rest because I've arranged a meeting with Dr. Gayle Hampshire first thing in the morning to break the news of Andrea's family."

"I'm sure she will not tolerate not seeing her mom much longer without an explanation," Lynn said by means of agreeing that talking with a psychologist was a great idea.

"That news will undoubtedly cause her much distress and cause her to need many meetings with Dr. Gayle. She is in a very weakened state right now, and this is going to dump more stress on her. During the next many sessions, hopefully, the subject will center on the fact that she was raped. We've not gotten a lot of information about her ordeal in the orchard. We may never, but pregnancy is another major concern at this juncture."

* * *

Andi was very agitated at her confinement, very sore everywhere on her body, and very upset that they, the hospital personnel, were keeping her from seeing her mom. How dare they. Being almost eighteen years of age might have made her almost an adult, but that didn't mean she didn't need or want her mom. She was sniffing back more tears when Lynn walked into the room at eight ten the next morning.

Lynn wasn't doing much better in the tears department. They seemed to be her constant companion since yesterday, but she entered the room chipper and ready to be with Andi even though she knew this was going to be a very hard day.

Without much more time for a kiss on the cheek and a smile for Andi, Dr. Harkness came in with a short, mature, attractive woman. "Good morning, ladies. Today, I have with me Dr. Gayle Hampshire, and we want to jump right into a few facts and explanations to help"—he looked straight at Andi now—"you, Andi, with some very upsetting news."

Stepping back, Dr. Harkness helped Lynn sit closer to Andi's bedside while Dr. Gayle spoke softly to Andi to make sure she had her eye contact and full attention. Stepping closer to Andi, she started with a simple statement.

"Andrea, I'm sorry to be the one to tell you that your mom can't come to be with you, because there was a fire at your house last night, and she perished, along with everyone else in the house. I mean everyone. They died of smoke inhalation while they slept. You, young lady, for some reason that needs further investigation and discussion, were not in the house, and therefore not affected by the conditions happening there."

Lynn, still holding Andi's hands down in her lap, looked back at Dr. Harkness, not wanting to see Andi's immediate reaction when realization hit.

Andi's skin got hot and itchy, and she started to shake. "Lynn, please tell me it's a lie. What is she talking about? Where is Mom? Today is Abby's birthday, and I almost missed it being here. Please, take me home…please," she pleaded.

With that, a new flood of tears started. Andi started scratching herself everywhere.

Carol rushed into the room and automatically started rubbing her daughter's shoulders for moral support because those shoulders were just asked for a favor she could not do. Carol also noticed the skin irritation was all over Andi's body and that she was going to be needing some sort of immediate medical attention.

Lynn was immobile, just trying to hold Andi's hands still from scratching and from drawing blood from her scratching. Things went from bad to worse quickly when Officer Stricker walked into the room, looking like he was silently reviewing his questions in his head. Lynn immediately and, with no room for discussion, demanded him to leave and not come back until he had doctors' permission to ask Andi his set of questions, which were going to require her to think and remember and feel her ordeal all over again. No, those questions had to wait.

Both doctors now needed to attend to Andi. The skin irritation and subsequent scratching had brought on an immediate fever, and the shock of the news rendered Andi unconsciousness again. Lynn and her mom were leaning against the wall in stark fear.

Andi met consciousness again with such fierce grief and longing that her screams could be heard down the hall. "Mom…Mom… Dad! *No…no!*" But that was short-lived as she passed out again.

Dr. Gayle conferred with Dr. Harkness briefly to make sure her sedative was not going to interfere with his steroid shot for the extreme case of hives which were very swollen and covered in blood. Dr. Harkness ordered a nurse to make Andrea comfortable and provide a sponge bath. Lynn and Carol left the room to get some coffee.

Facts

Not wanting to leave the hospital without some information, Office Stricker found Jeff Marsden in a waiting room just down the hall and started to engage him in conversation.

Pleasantries established, he started with his questions.

"Mr. Marsden, what time did your daughter get home after the concert Saturday night? Did you know the young man driving the car?"

Jeff, taken a little aback by the swift change of direction, informed the officer, to the best of his knowledge, the end time of the concert and party time at Joan Carpenter's house. Then they drove home in the company of her boyfriend, Tom Often. Jake Hobart was Andrea's boyfriend, and he was driving his car.

Officer Stricker thanked Jeff profusely for his exact information. It was the most information he'd gotten so far. Now he had times and names. He could find addresses and really start talking with the people who were there.

"Damn, the day is going away from me," Jim mumbled as he pulled in front of the Hobart home at 11:10 a.m. on Sunday. He had made a quick stop at the station to make a note of Jake's home address and Tom Often's as well. Mrs. Hobart was in residence, but Jake was not. She offered the information that after breakfast that morning, Jake had headed to Fayetteville to his buddy's house to meet him for a few rounds of handball at the SwingTime Ball Center.

"What is this about, Officer?" she inquired. Upon hearing the news of the tragedy at the Chambers home and the fact that Andrea was in the hospital, Mrs. Hobart grabbed her number finder, ran to her hall telephone, and started dialing a number, all the while telling Officer Stricker she had no knowledge of the fire, and she doubted Jake did either. "He'll want to go to Andi immediately," she said, looking sadly stricken and dialing the phone.

"Hi, Pete, is Jake with you?"

"Yes, Mrs. Hobart, he's right here. We just got back from the center. Hold on" was the reply at the other end.

"Hi, Ma, what's up?" With relief at hearing his voice, she offered the phone to Officer Stricker. After he introduced himself, he started off with his questions. Mrs. Hobart looked on with concern and fright.

"Were you with Andrea last night?"

"Yes, sir. I dropped her off at her house about one a.m."

"Did you actually see her enter the house? Did you walk her to the door?"

"Sir, what is this all about? Why the questions. Is Andi all right?"

"Jake, there was a fire at the Chambers residence discovered long after you left Andi, and Andi was not in her room. She could not be found anywhere in the house. Did she have plans of going anywhere else after you left her?"

"No, I had her to her door at curfew time, and I'm sure she wouldn't defy her folks by going back out. How bad is the house? Did you look everywhere for Andi?" Fighting back a guilty conscience at his state of inebriation, he had to ask questions of concern.

Jake asked if there was anything he could do to assist in finding Andi.

"We needed to call in support from neighboring towns to help in fighting the fire, but to no avail. It was a total loss. Andi was found a few hours later and is in the hospital from unrelated fire injuries."

"What hospital? I want to see her, make sure she's all right." Jake sounded genuinely concerned.

Officer Striker told him to call Winthrop General before going up there to make sure she could accept company. There were doctors and tests scheduled, so he should check first.

With that, Jake ran out to his car, yelling back, "Gotta go, Pete! An accident or fire or something at Andi's house has put her in the hospital. Call ya later!"

Sitting alone in his own car, Jake took a minute to try and think clearly about the events of the night before. He had been such an ass. He knew it. She deserved better than that, better than him. But a guy wants what he wants!

Before heading out of town, Jake headed to Speer Street to see for himself. There were still many fire trucks and men roaming around the yard and neighborhood. He drove slowly past the shell of the house, turned around, and headed back down the hill. *Holy shit*, he thought. When had that started? He ran through the night before in his head. *Forget it. She's better off without me. Poor kid. There is no way I can have her or help her now.*

Now traveling out of town, wouldn't you know, he caught the only red light. Stretching his hand to his neatly combed light brown sun-streaked hair and checking it in the rearview mirror, he noticed, first, his bandaged hand. Handball injury. Quick thinking on his part. He patted his hair in place and relaxed again. Winthrop was always a busy place, but he learned his way around last year with his mother's confinement with a gallbladder surgery and his father's death three years ago. Today, parking should be relatively easy, and finding Andi in emergency would be easy as well.

I need to apologize to her for being such a cad last night and just generally be nice and better to her because of her family, he thought as he was walking down the same tan hallways Lynn had walked down a few minutes earlier. But he was thinking, *Her kiss, her smile, her easy way with everyone she meets, she's more than just a great body. Please, God, let her be okay.*

Wake-Up Call

Kevin was unaccustomed to waking up alone. Never before was he alone in the back seat of Betsy, under a bridge with the only sunbeam in sight streaming into a window straight in his eyes. "Where the hell am I?" he mumbled. "Oh, my head. What the hell. Where did the blood come from?" He had reached up to rub his eyes and saw the patches of blood on his hands.

Now a little nervous about what he couldn't remember, he got out of the car, straightened his clothes, took a deep breath, and resumed driving until he saw a diner flashing open. The counter had only four men eating breakfast, so he asked about a men's room. He got directions. "At the end of the counter, take a left."

When he returned with clean hands, face, and combed hair, he also sat at the counter with coffee and the morning newspaper. He had drunk too much last night, his head hurt, and he had no idea how he drove himself. That's right, he drove himself. He felt a little guilty running out on Rockwell. Now he remembered the orchard! The girl. He was in the orchard. Rockwell never showed up. Kevin opened the paper and saw a headline: "Grafton house fire, two other towns responding. Look for the full story in our evening edition."

No, couldn't be. He wouldn't do that. Where the hell is he? Do I go back and look for him? I can't ask anyone. No one knows we were there.

No one knows we were coming here. What if someone saw my car? What if my Maryland plates ring a bell with someone? What if the girl saw me? No…no way. All of these thoughts were going through his hurting head and making his stomach ache.

Kevin couldn't even finish his coffee. He left a buck on the counter and left the diner. His car couldn't get him out of this god-forsaken area fast enough. *Slow down…Maryland plates speeding, fast car, alone, nervous, no, don't get stopped.* With a great effort for the next fifteen minutes, until he saw signs for the Mass Pike, he drove like an old lady. Once on the pike heading west toward New York, he stepped on it. Betsy gave him a good ride!

The apartment was such a welcome sight. He took a shower, four aspirin, a shot and a beer, then straight to bed. Nervousness, exhaustion, confusion, and a wicked hangover led to restless sleep, but sleep he did for the next twenty-four hours. Once awake, the confusion was still there. Wednesday couldn't come fast enough. Then Rockwell could explain what the hell he did and where he'd been. But Wednesday came, and still no Rockwell. He was becoming very concerned and confused as to what to do next or who he could talk to. He, for his own preservation, decided he could talk to no one! He needed to know more than he did now, so the library felt like a good place to start.

Looking through the most recent periodicals and asking for newspapers from other states, he had a pile to look through until he came to the *Worcester Evening Gazette* dated April 16, 1964. Top headline didn't interest him, but the article in the bottom right corner entitled HOUSE FIRE STILL A MYSTERY had his full attention. He did not quite believe what he was reading. He read on about the seven bodies carried out of the house, seven lives lost due to smoke inhalation, and one unidentified body burned beyond recognition found out by the garage. Anyone with information about this tragedy was asked to call…

With his heart broken and his brain not wanting to comprehend or believe what he had read, he headed back to the apartment to try and sort out his feelings. He became depressed and reclusive. He still waited for the next Wednesday, and the one after that, and the one after that. He knew he was the weak link in their relationship. Rockwell always had the ideas and the lead, but they always stayed together and knew where the other was. This was totally out of character and unsettling. He knew he had to do something more than sit around and mope and brood. If he really believed the eighth body was not Rockwell, he needed to do something, anything, to try and find him. So he put on his thinking cap and came up with what he thought was the perfect next move.

Kevin went into the student union (the university lunchroom) where over the last three or so weeks, he had spent a good deal of time and posted Missing posters of Rockwell Sabers.

In two weeks, there had been no results, and no one saw Rockwell.

It was time to go home.

His folks were beside themselves when he came waltzing into the dining room for dinner on this quiet Thursday night. They asked all the questions that he knew they would ask, and he had mentally tried to anticipate and have answers for those questions but failed miserably.

His next visit was over to the Sabers to see Rockwell's folks and get the same barrage of questions. But when he got there, of course, Captain Sabers wasn't home. Sitting with Mrs. Sabers and Rachel was very uncomfortable. The pictures Rockwell had shared with him were still in the back seat of his car. That's were his mind kept going. *Keep his secret…keep his secret* kept crossing his mind.

"Mrs. Sabers, I posted a missing person poster at school, hoping someone there might have seen him, but that got no response. So I think it is now time to call the police and report a missing person."

When Kevin left the house, he could breathe a little deeper until he looked at the pictures in the bag again. For years, he had had a crush on Rachel. He thought she was the most beautiful girl in the world, but she was Rockwell's sister, which meant hands off. *Stop thinking about her.*

But now, seeing her again, he searched in the bag of pictures for two particular ones he remembered seeing, the girl at the top of the hill, the one he had in the orchard. Sure enough…she looked just like Rachel!

Aspen

After two and half months in a rehab facility, because she needed the counseling and medical care and really had nowhere else to go, Andi felt strong enough to move into an apartment with Lynn. Lynn supported her through the funerals of her family and psychological struggles with her pregnancy, which was now the biggest part of her life. Andi thought back to only a few months ago when she thought, *We're graduating. It's the beginning of the rest of our lives.*

Mrs. Amy Madeline Chambers, daughter of 1938 Nobel Prize winner Dr. Martin P. Samson and Judith R. Samson of Clearway, Virginia, her oldest son Aaron, twins Alley and Alex, Adam, and Abby were laid to rest in a family plot in the cemetery just two streets over from their house. Captain Aspen Chambers was declared dead by forensic means and dental records by a military autopsy performed at the Portsmouth Naval facility in New Hampshire. He was laid to rest with the family with military honors. There were military dignitaries present. Andrea Chambers

was the only member of the family not home at
the time of the fire and still resides in Fisherville.

The obituary was short and to the point because Andi had very little to add. Her family's background was cut short and not a big conversation piece around her house. Her mom's dad was a Nobel Prize winner in 1938 due to his contribution to the strength of steel when mixed with an epoxy element and put under pressure, etc. The technique was patented and won him great notoriety. All of his work was done for a naval base in Virginia, where he had top security clearance while working for Higgins & Platen. His work was always under a gag order. (That was a term Andi learned and heard many times in her dad's house.) Dr. Samson and his wife of twenty-two years lost their lives in a plane crash returning from Switzerland in 1940 when Amy was only thirteen. Being an only child and being left by a man of means, Amy never had a money worry. All of her inheritance was handled by attorneys appointed by her dad in a trust that was set up at the time of his awards.

Amy was sent to a girls' finishing school set up by the executor of Martin Samson's estate until she was eighteen years old. Always being herded around with fifteen other girls, eating at the same table at the same time with the same fifteen girls, but always returning to her lonely private room in the dorm, Amy was ready and groomed for independence at her next birthday. She was awarded a sum of $18K per year for her personal and educational needs. Amy left that situation, looking forward to her next chapter. To actually build a life and experience new and wonderful things. Having never been on her own before, she was accepted at and jumped at the chance to go to a coed college in Norfolk, Virginia.

The school was huge, the city busy and bustling, and the pace mesmerizing. Her academic schedule left little time for socializing, so when she was invited to go to Jean's house (her roommate) for the long Thanksgiving weekend, she accepted with pleasure. It was a real home with a mom and dad and two younger brothers. A real family and home-cooked meals. What a treat. And it was. Amy commented often to Jean that, that was what she had missed growing up, and someday, that was what she wanted. A house, a real home with kids, and that white proverbial fence. Jean thought she was nuts, but with her looks (and money), it wouldn't take her long to snag a guy.

Winter Slender Ball was in three weeks, and both girls needed to spruce up their wardrobe if they intended to catch the eye of any available or interesting young men. Their shopping trip was successful and tiring, so they stopped at an outdoor coffee wagon and sat on the wall behind it.

Jean and Amy were always looking at guys, at men of all sizes, tall and short, light hair, dark hair, well-dressed or even wearing hats.

"That guy, that one over there, real tall, wide shoulders with gorgeous black hair and a tiny round butt," said Amy with a sigh. She was still staring at him, leaning against the pole at the malt shop.

Jean chuckled. "I said pick out a guy you could bring home to mother and then mold him into what you want. That guy, never. He comes off too sure of himself. Besides, he looks too old for you."

"Hmmm...a mature man...why not? I know how to lead. Watch and learn." Feeling bold, she strode off in his direction.

Jean did just that. She watched and learned as her friend with her short curly bob the color of the sun and those green eyes that sparkled like neon with white specs (just like her father's, she said) and a figure unmatched in any girly magazine caught Mr. Handsome's attention and proceeded to engage him in a flirtatious conversation.

"Well done," Jean said when Amy came bouncing back, all excited.

"We made a date for tomorrow afternoon, a river ride down to Pikes Dam and then hot dogs at Hal's Stand on Maple Road."

"So tell me his name. Where does he go to school? How old is he? What time is your date?" Jean couldn't get the questions out fast enough.

"Ummm…I don't know how old he is. He's not in school. He's military. He loves my hair. We are meeting at the North Park Gate tomorrow at two and…ummmm, I never asked his name. We never got around to introductions."

The next day, Sunday, Amy was at North Park Gate at precisely 2:00 p.m. She was over-the-top excited, trying not to pace or look too worried he wouldn't show. He had to come. He had to live up to her dreamy anticipation of him. It was a splendid day for a boat ride. There was no way he could let her down. Then, with a sinking heart, she saw him talking to a ravishing blond, way out of her league, and her wishful thoughts sunk. She turned, so with her back to the oncoming road, she didn't see his approach. And approach he did with open arms and a greeting hug. *Whoa*, she thought, returning the hug, trying not to melt in his arms. She was very startled in a good way. Amy took a half step back from him, still touching his arms, looked up into his clear blue/gray eyes, and said, "Hi, I'm Amy."

"I knew with that hair, you'd have a short choppy name. Amy suits you." He took her hand, and they walked to the ticket counter and proceeded to board the boat.

Many minutes passed as they sat side by side, watching other people take their seats, listening to several conversations all at once with music starting and announcements being made. Amy's excitement at sitting next to and holding hands with this man—yes, man, she decided—had her heart thumping so hard she thought for sure everyone around them could hear. Finally getting up the nerve, she turned to him and asked, "Who was that beautiful blond that had your attention?"

"I won't lie to you. She's an old flame, one that has burned out. I'm sure you've had plenty in your life that just…faded away."

"Not really. So back to us. What is your name?"

Still holding her hand, he turned a little in his seat and reached for her other hand. He smiled, looking directly into her upturned face, and said, "Chambers. Aspen Chambers has finally been born because of you."

The afternoon was grand, but later that night…

"Shit, shit, shit. I've done it again. I want her. What have I done? Walk away. Walk away, fool. What have I done? Shit, shit, shit! Think…Clear…I'll need her again. Boy, she did it before. She enjoys the barrel she's put me under. I guess I'll just stay there a little longer. She's a pretty good lay. She sure knows how to pull strings and rearrange lives. Shit, shit, shit."

With his head in his hands, he just sat thinking, *What in the hell was she doing here today? Is she my bad penny or my saving grace? Of all the people for Amy to pick out…why was she there?*

"Aspen Chambers. Captain Aspen Chambers…sounds good. She can make it happen. She's done it before. Who am I, really?"

When he got to back to base in Norfolk, his first visit was to CC Clear with his urgent request for her assistance, the kind that cost him a lifetime of intrigue and mystery but got him the girl. He had the stamina and guts to pull off this scam. She had the rank and insatiable desire to push the envelope and own the barrel. Her bucket list could never include children, so their tie remained, him unquestionably jumping through hoops of her desire.

So in February 1944, the new Aspen made Amy Madeline his wife, and they set up housing off base in Norfolk, Virginia. He was happy. He knew he wanted more children in his life. Now it could happen. He just needed to remember where he was and who he was with. That was what made him…him!

And time went on.

Inheritance

The cause of the fire was still unknown and still under investigation by the state fire marshal and town fire officials. The means by which she became pregnant were a nagging memory and an unsolved crime according to the police, but it was now a way of life for Andi and ever supportive Lynn. The two young women worked tirelessly at the apartment to make it a home to welcome a baby into. Lynn decided to go to school locally to help out with Andi and be around when the baby was born.

Andi really hated to be alone. She really never had been, but circumstances like this forced the quiet and the thoughts and the memories to surface. When she left the hospital, eighteen and pregnant, she needed to face facts as presented by her family's attorneys. She didn't even know she had attorneys. She didn't know she was the end of the bloodline on both sides of the family and to inherit everything her folks owned. She had no idea what was to come from her mom's father's estate.

All the large insurance policies and moneys were in her mom's name. She was told most of the money was old money that had multiplied many times over from her grandfathers' estate left to her mother and now to her.

The smaller insurance portions were many policies obtained from her father's military past, from her dad's war bonds, or other secret cash holdings. Andi received two pieces of correspondence from a Major CC Clear with regrets, condolences, and checks. This finalized the connections to his military career.

She had no idea she was a millionairess. Andrea's inheritance was a huge surprise to her, just something she never thought about.

Christmas was really hard on Andi that year, but Lynn's parents tried their best to make it a festive day and filled her broken heart with thoughts of the coming of her own baby and baby toys, clothes, holiday food, and the most needed car seat. They were really such good people, and she loved them dearly.

Winter that year was a bear. January, with its biting winds and sleety rains, made everything icy and miserable. Maddie made her appearance on one of those sleety rainy nights, and Andi hoped it wasn't a forbearance of the future with her beautiful little girl. She had hoped that her nasty, negative attitude would change once her child was born, so why was that her first thought? Lynn had talked to doctors and brought her books on attitude training and depression and was trying so hard to make a happy home to welcome Maddie into, if only Andi could see the good around her like she used to.

The next few years, Maddie grew into a silly, happy, playful kid who loved her mother and her auntie Lynn when she was around. Lynn maintained her room in the apartment but spent most of her time at the university and with her beloved Chuck. Chuck and Mr. Marsden were the only male figures in Maddie's life, and she loved them both. Andi grew stronger and more self-assured, more like the old Andi who loved kids and noise and activities around her. Finishing her degree was a monumental effort, but she achieved it with the support from Lynn and Chuck and the Marsdens and good grades. To fill her life with what she felt she lost, she enrolled both herself and Maddie in a daytime facility where Maddie could spend her days sharing and learning and start the beginnings of beautiful memories. During this time, Andi was enrolled, down the hall, in physiological crime related courses toward her master's. Weeks turned into months into years, and Andi was now a full-fledged doctor of criminal behavior. She had passed her strenuous course at the police academy and also held her police badge proudly.

BOOK 2

5 Lost Road

Rockwell, age twenty-two, second oldest son of Rhonda and Reginald, resided on 5 Lost Road, Towson, Maryland, with his five other siblings. Rockwell was six-foot-one with curly black hair always worn short because of the curls. He had wide shoulders, thinning down to a narrow waist, with long skinny legs. He had thick glasses. He was waiting for the day to get corrective surgery to shuck the glasses and become a most handsome him! More like his older brother Russell, always the stud and never the student! For him, it was money for college. Not contact lenses or corrective surgery, just college. Rockwell was always doing this or that for someone else, always the pleaser, as his mom would say. He was good kid, attentive son, great older brother, and excellent student. He just graduated college, four years at Rensselaer Polytechnic Institute, or RPI, in Troy, New York. He pulled a 4.0 for the last three years. Always the student, never the stud!

* * *

At first, growing up in a not quite city, Towson, Maryland, was fun for me and my big brother Russell. We would go everywhere with dad. I was really little, so his shoulders were always my favorite seat. The world looked so big to me way up there. Dad was a military man. He said that made him big and strong. He was always that to me. He and Russell were my heroes. Then we had a girl. Dad said it was mom's turn to have fun. He had us two, and mom only had Rachel. It was two against one!

It was just about then that my world opened up and got so much bigger. I started first grade. Mom said it's uncanny that I had memories going so far back, but I do. I remember lots of things. For so long, I remember watching Russell leaving the yard to go to Hamm's house to play without me. That was down our shared drive-way…four houses long and across the street. We lived on a dead-end street. Mom said they were the safest. Hamm was Russell's best friend and one year older than him! They could go a lot of places together.

My school was my fun place. Once the twins were born, I called school my safe haven. That was the year the Schaffers moved in three houses down, still in our driveway. Mom called it our dead-end road. As long as I stayed in the driveway, I was allowed a little more freedom.

I remember the moving truck backing to the front door of the tan house that had been empty for so long. The two men got out of the truck, unhinged the back door, and just sat there, smoking their cigarettes. They weren't doing anything, so I went to talk to them to be neighborly. They were waiting for the owners of this house to show up and unlock the door so they could move the furniture in. I was full of questions, and they were really nice. I found out a boy about my age was moving in. I didn't budge. I sat right there on the grass and waited for the family to show up with the keys and their boy.

I hadn't sat there long, and Mom showed up, smelling really good for a late Thursday afternoon. She bummed a couple of cigarettes from the tall guy and just pushed the twins' stroller back and forth and visited with them until a car drove up. The car stopped by the truck. My mom said her goodbyes to the movers, told me not to get in the way, and she strolled off. I hated it when Mom smoked. I didn't hug her anymore. Her hair and clothes stunk.

It was my turn to have a best friend and not want to be with and follow Russell everywhere he went, so I continued to wait. When the car stopped, a guy about my age was just as anxious to get out of the car as I was for him to do so. He saw me and said, "HI, I'm Kevin." And that's all it took. Fast friends. From that day on, we did everything together.

Kevin's mom and dad were okay. They supported him in everything he did. Thank goodness for his dad. He played backyard games and basketball in the driveway with us and transported us to T-ball and Cub Scouts. My dad was never around for these things. Always on duty, he'd say. He was rather attached to the Army. Whatever "attached" meant.

Life in my house growing up always seemed so regimented with mom's schedules. I even remember when we got our first TV. Sunday nights, no matter what, it was always *Bonanza*, then Mom would go out back to smoke her cigarettes while everyone took their showers before school the next day.

Dad tried to be home every three weeks for four days, then he'd be off again. It never failed. Two days before Dad got home, it was do this or do that, clean there, wash that. For Dad's time home, the house was squeaky clean. Our suppers were also better. For those four days, Mom relaxed her schedule a bit and always looked her best for Dad. My mom was a very pretty woman. All my friends thought so.

When I was a little older, I realized that for those three weeks Dad was away, our house was run like a military operation, with everyone's schedules listed on the refrigerator. First, Mom's Monday night bowling, Rachel home with the twins, and on Tuesday and Thursday nights, Russell worked, which meant Mom needed to be available to pick him up by nine thirty (from wherever she had gone off to). Wednesday, Mom shopping; Friday, Mom painting class; Saturday morning, Mom out with Ruby and Rose for their dance class. It seemed like Mom was never home.

Unlike at Kevin's house, we never had Sunday dinner with family. We didn't have any. There were no relatives on Dad's side of the family. He spoke of his parents passing just once when he was just out of high school, and he was an only child. Mom was disinherited from her family when she married Dad. I remember her telling us that story. It wasn't really sad. She made it sound romantic. So really, she only had us.

Looking back, Dad didn't do much for us. He certainly didn't give Mom much. We lived in a two-bedroom bungalow at the end of a dirt dead-end road. It was the only dead-end road in our town, which was just a little bit outside of a big city. Our kitchen was big with a big round table with a round lazy Susan in the middle holding salt and pepper, a butter dish, a sugar bowl, and napkins. It was always dirty. The floor had broken linoleum tiles and was covered with throw rugs. The best feature was the picture window at the back of the kitchen looking into the wooded backyard. Mom always complained that that wall should have had additional cabinets for storage, but I loved that window. It was also always dirty.

Mom had the biggest room in the house. Her bedroom door was always locked. We never could go in there. It was probably dirty as well.

Russel and I shared a small room with bunk beds. I was on top. There was a trunk at the foot of the bed that was Russell's. It was always locked (I'm a snoop), and there was a short chest of drawers on the opposite wall from the closet. We each had a side. Mine was always neater than his.

Then came the girl. Rachel had it pretty good for a while. She got to bed in with Mom in that big room. She was about three when I got to sleep on the top bunk in my room. Dad was coming home for his four days, so Russell would go to Hamm's house to sleep. I got moved to the top bunk, but Rachel had to come and sleep on the bottom bunk. It wasn't so bad. This made me the big brother. This went on for a few years until the twins were born. Now the twins were in with Mom all the time and Rachel in with me. By this time, Russel had made himself a "man pad" in the basement. It solved some sleeping problems. He stayed down there every night.

It got so Dad's coming home was an inconvenience. It changed all the sleeping arrangements. But Mom said it worked in her favor because we got to buy a new living room couch, one that opened into a bed. So when Dad came home, the twins were on the couch in the living room, not in their room. The old couch got moved down to Russel's man pad, which thrilled him to bits.

The living room was long and narrow, the entire length of the house on the front of the house. It's cathedral ceiling was lined with light-colored wooden planks highlighting the woodland motif of the room, with its tan wainscoting paneling to chair-rail height and textured wood look wallpaper. It was an attractive room, the one that

spoke to Mom and Dad years back when they were looking to buy...
so they bought the house.

The new couch filled the entirety of the back wall. It's too bad
its flowery print didn't match the other chairs in the room, which
were blue and brown plaid. Nearly the entire front wall was glass,
allowing sunlight and warmth to beam in. It also highlighted the
cobwebs in the center peak of the cathedral and was also always dirty.

The one thing I remember hearing Dad say was that he needed
his privacy in this own home. He didn't need a big house, just one
room to share, only with his wife when he was here. So Mom made
that happen.

But now came Riley. Another little boy was brought home to
the house that was already busting at the seams with kids. I was about
ten that summer when Dad came home for a week. But rather than
staying home with all of us and Mom, he took me and Russell on a
road trip. Just us men. It was the best vacation I'd ever had with my
dad. Even Russell acted like a good big brother.

Road Trip

After a long time driving, we stopped and bought burgers and fries. We were told not to eat yet and got back in the car. We stopped just a few turns later, up the road near a bridge and a great grassy patch. We sat on the grass, had our lunch, and just talked to Dad about everything. When we finished eating, he went to the trunk of the car and pulled out...fishing poles. This was a side of Dad we didn't know. He seemed happy to be spending time with us. We fished off the bridge until dark. We just stayed there and fished and continued talking. (I'd love to find that back road again. That was the life...peaceful and simple.) We picked up the area we had occupied for the last few hours, trash from our lunch, all the fishing line that got caught in bushes and low tree limbs trying to cast out, stomped down the earth we disturbed looking for worms, got back in the car.

"Now what?" said Dad. "I'm open for suggestions. What do you guys want to do? We've got a whole week...I know," he said with excitement in his voice. Now he sounded like one of the guys, so we sat back to find out what was next.

We didn't know what was next, except a short ride later, we were pulling into a Harry Handy Mart.

"Okay," said Dad. "What clothes did you guys bring for the week? You'll need a bathing suit, sneakers, clean underwear, of course.

I don't care what you sleep in. Unless you do, a few T-shirts, pick up two pairs of jeans, a light jacket, and hurry up. When we are done here, we'll eat. I'm starved!"

* * *

Russell and Rockwell looked at each other like "Who is this guy?" They agreed they liked him a lot better than the man who showed up every three weeks. He went into their mom's bedroom and only came out to eat. But they were hungry too, so after a quick but comprehensive run through the store, they had all that their dad said to get and more. Rockwell found two of the books that were on his summer reading list and put them in the basket. He also picked up an all-in-one camera with twenty-five-color ready-to-go exposures. Mail it in when full…presto…color prints. Russell also picked up one of those cameras and a poster of Danish blond bombshell Britt Semand to liven up his man pad. He didn't know who she was, but she sure was pretty. Dad didn't blink an eye. He paid for everything and told Russell he had good taste in women.

Back in the car, they found out that they had driven out of Maryland, through a little of New Jersey, and they were currently in a corner of New York. So far, they'd had a busy day. The next motel they saw, their dad made a crazy turn, and they were parked at the vacancy sign. Once registered, they walked across the lot to an all-night diner. Their dad said these places were always close to a motel and had the best food. The boys were excited.

The day just seemed to get better and better. Rockwell had never experienced anything like it. After they ate, they were back in their room watching TV, their choice of program, which was an oddity. They were waiting for a cot to be brought to the room as it had only two beds. Dad said he'd take the cot as he wanted the boys to get a good night's rest. After everyone took a shower, the TV went off, lights went off, and it was time to sleep. Rockwell never remembered sleeping better.

Secure that the boys were sound asleep, Reginald made his escape. He left a note taped to the TV saying STEPPED OUT FOR A DRINK. BE BACK SOON. With that accomplished, he slipped the motel key in his beach robe pocket and slipped out the door.

One minute later and four doors down, his welcome was expressed by roaming hands swiftly inside his robe. One was rounding his manly shaft and the other fondling his tight round ass.

He was accustomed to this. He was quickly down her throat with kisses only practice could provide and hands working the hard rigid nipples standing atop very large, very round, nice firm breasts. They were nearly breathless, now standing toe to toe.

"I thought you'd never get here I've been playing, but all by myself…with myself. I am so ready for you," she coyly said.

With that, he picked her up, laid her on the bed with legs slightly spread, and began fingering her curls just above her shiny wet center.

"I'll be the judge of your readiness," he whispered as he spread the lovely wet sex lips. He lowered his head and began his investigation. First, the right lip was licked clean and smooth, and the then the left. He did not need to hold her lips apart any longer, and his fingers were itching to slide into her tight wet opening and gently slide along the moist, slippery walls of her vagina, always in search of the spot that made her crave more, scream with pleasure, and twist her body in some of the most unlikely of ways. His tongue, by this time, was needing some sucking and licking, so again their mouths came together in a most intoxicatingly sexy way. Their bodies were now touching lengthwise, with hands touching everywhere and mouths busy pushing the limit. His penis was looking for action. Just then, it was sliding into her, filling her pussy and teasing that illusive spot that gave way to waves of extreme pleasure. It almost felt like pain. During the best of times, this orgasm lasted a couple of minutes but could be reactivated by the merest touch, sometimes lightly to the clitoris, a sensitive nipple, or a kiss with the tongue just slightly probing and probing again and again. And before you know it, the bed sheets are wound tightly in her fists because the waves were so intense, they drove her to screams.

"You never cease to amaze me," he sighed while caressing her face with his two hands. He thought, *There are times I'm glad she can't have children.*

Then one minute later and four doors down, he was alone on his stiff lonely cot, listening to his boys sleep deeply.

Sunday

The next day, there was another two-hour ride, this time north to New Hampshire. They stopped at another motel in Wolfeboro, where they were setting up for two days. Again, the room had two queen-size beds. This time, after the boys broke out of their little huddle, they agreed that they could sleep together in one bed, and Dad could have the other rather than sleeping on a cot. It could work. It was still more comfortable than home.

Lake Winnipesaukee was huge, more like the ocean, Russell thought, but he'd never seen the ocean. When he touched the water, it was warm and reflected the sun on its surface. The boys had never had an outing quite like this. They made friends with a family they met walking on a pier and spent the afternoon on the beach, swimming and getting to know them. The water was wonderful. Rockwell swam out to a dock with his new friends and couldn't believe how far down he could see. He saw crawfish walking on the bottom of the lake, at least eight feet down. That's how clean the water was! The pond they went to at home wasn't clean like this. He didn't know clean lakes like this existed. When he got back to his dad and the blanket, he found cookout plans were made with this family for their first night.

They were back at the motel to get cleaned up for the cookout. Russell reached into his Harry's bag for a new T-shirt and felt the camera at the bottom

"Hey, Rockwell, have you taken any pictures? I forget all about my camera. How about you?"

Rockwell was bummed. He had wanted a picture of every motel they stayed at so that he could make a picture report of every place they'd stopped and stayed and put miles and activities for each place.

"It's too bad I didn't get a picture of the first motel, but I can start my trip report there after Dad reminds me where that was. I just remember that we went fishing. I've never done that before."

The cookout with new friends, lots of new friends, loud music, and yard games went well into the night. Both boys remembered to take pictures. The best ones were of the dads playing horseshoes and chasing after the wayward shoes not thrown just right.

Russell enjoyed watching the women in their bathing suits bend over to pick up the horseshoes and hand them off to the next player. He also loved the one named Crystal, who handed off to him and this guy Jim ice-cold beers from the tub on the ground. She kissed him on the cheek, butt checked him and, told them to get lost for a while. This was the coolest thing! So off they went. Totally out of sight, he and Jim sat with their backs up against a tree, drank their beers, and totally told lies about themselves. Russell thought, *Why not? I'm never gonna see this guy again.* So for now he was fourteen years old, in high school, and wishing his dad hadn't caught him with the cigarettes and taken them away, because he loved to smoke when he had a beer.

Exhaustion slammed into the boys the minute they were in the room. Lights out and bed. Sleep was instantaneous. Reginald taped the same note to the TV and once again made his escape.

The second day started later in the morning as everyone needed to sleep in to rejuvenate. This day also flew by with as much activity as the first. They finished this day with steaks on the grill out the back door of their motel room with the people in the next room. Rockwell took his pictures of the motel, even the size of the steak he had for dinner. Before lights out that night, both boys studied their cameras intensely. Okay, twenty-five exposures, four pictures already taken, four days left. They had five pictures a day left in the cameras, maybe with one to spare. That was going to be a special picture, one of them with Dad on each camera. When they had that figured out to their satisfaction, it was lights out and again, instant sleep.

Reginald looked at his two boys, content to know that they were enjoying themselves and still naïve enough for him to be able to leave the room like this with them unaware. Taping the same note to the TV, Reginald left and met Crystal in her room, as planned.

The unspoken promise of burying himself in her warm, wet, waiting golden triangle of pleasure made him wet and feeling like a boy again. She had that effect on him. Tonight would be no different.

Just knowing that Crystal's favors were as close as a closed door away made him weak with unspent desire. Watching her turn hot dogs, tend to steaks, chug at a longneck beer, stretch out on the chaise lounge, and send him looks that were just for him…well… made him. They played well together. There was no way that these new friends knew they had it all planned out to meet here.

She was very good at giving him what he craved. She helped him with his marriage to Rhonda. She knew these were his boys.

She knew playing with him this way was dangerous. She knew she got under his skin with the stunt she pulled with Russell, but he was powerless with her. She had what he wanted. She made herself available any time for him, like these two days, under his sons' noses. She held out for him to…reach…to touch…to fondle, but not to take unless she said so. And when she unleashed, he was powerless to resist or refuse. There were times when she was unavailable or just out of reach and made him beg. But that was part of her barrel. She owned it, used it, and kept him under it!

She'd been in this game with him long enough to know what waiting for him was like. Years of learning about his wife and kids and his life made what they had an invigorating sex life for him and a no lose deal for her. Crystal was not cut out for marriage, to stay at home and cook and clean and do laundry. That didn't work. Just great sex when she wanted! Games by her rules made her life fun. His were hectic at times. She saw to it. That's what made it fun. He knew Crystal's method of cajoling. A phone call and he needed to make it happen, whatever she wanted. Otherwise, the wife would find out. Those were the rules she had set up many years ago. She knew his schedule at the base and his time home. Damn those four days. She'd always threatened with the wife card but never acted upon it. Yet… was always the question? He'd not disappointed her yet, either in bed or showing up where and when she wanted him. So this outing with the boys…it was her doing.

Enjoy your boys, but fuck me!

Monday/Tuesday

The next morning, they were off to their next destination. but breakfast first.

On their way to the car, their dad said, "Ya know, boys, we are eating our way through this mini vacation like food is going out of style."

"I know, and I like it," commented Russell with a grin from ear to ear.

This time, they found a Cracker Barrel.

"It's a chain restaurant, but it's reputed to have excellent food. Wanna try it?" Dad asked.

"As long as you are paying, I'll eat anything," Rockwell snuck in.

After stuffing down an enormous breakfast of eggs, pancakes, hash browns, and sausage, they all agreed the food was excellent. Dad gave them each money and told them to take their time in the attached Country Store while he excused himself to head to the bathroom.

"What the hell…are you crazy? Here!" The ladies' room was blocked off with wet floor cones and closed chains.

Within five minutes, Reginald had been suffocated by two large beautiful breasts and had his mouth ravaged and filled with as many extremities as she could reach to it. He moved around or probed back and forth in it. All the while, she was stroking or sitting or bouncing or straddling his very ready-for-her, long, swollen, pulsing penis. He tucked in his shirt and just made it back to the table to ask the boys if they had enough time to pick out a neat souvenir.

They were back at the table to finish their drinks. "Russell added that the pancakes were the best, really great. Mom can't seem to cook them right." It was the only mention of their mom so far on this trip. By now, the boys were anxious to get going, but not before Rockwell took a picture of where they just ate breakfast.

The next jaunt was short, over to Hampton Beach. This was a very commercial area with arcades, water slides, roller rinks, saltwater taffy, fortune-tellers, bowling, and food stands. It had a carnival feeling. That was one side of the road. The other side was the Atlantic Ocean. With just a quick look around, Rockwell and Russell knew they were going to have another great day.

"Dad, how long are we staying here so I'll know what to do first?" Russell asked. All inhibitions were now out of both boys. Dad was laying it out for the taking, and that's what they did.

"How about two nights in the next motel we come across? I'll make sure it's within walking distance to all of this, but we eat good food, not this junk. Agreed?"

"This is what heaven must be like," said Rockwell. "I want to swim in the ocean and have lobster for supper," he continued.

Their dad agreed. "That's real food, all right. I'm in."

Russell turned green at the thought of eating lobster. "I'll eat chicken. You two can eat chicken of the sea. I'm not!" exclaimed Russell.

100

The next motel was very much like the others. Rockwell was getting used to this and loving every minute. Again, he and Russell were going to share a bed. It was no big deal!

They stowed their Harry bags on the top shelf of the closet, changed into bathing suits, grabbed their cameras and a motel towel, and headed for the beach. Rockwell couldn't wait to show Kevin the pictures he was taking of this vacation. It was the first time he'd thought about Kevin.

This first day was heaven-sent, except for the sunburn on Rockwell's forehead, shoulders, and tips of his ears. The summer sun was strong but didn't warm the water up much. The water was freezing, so swimming was minimal for Russell. But not for Rockwell. He loved it.

More than that, he learned to love the outdoor shower at the motel. He loved being naked outside in the warm air.

"Damn you, Russell. Bring my towel back!" Rockwell hollered when he saw the tip of the towel disappear over the wooden shower wall.

"This isn't funny. I don't have any clothes in here. Dad expects—"

His words stopped abruptly as he heard the giggling of girls as they whipped open his shower door and sprayed him with string-fetti. He was mortified, trying to cover his naked self, but he saw his dad waiting for the girls to turn around and see him!

Just then, he heard his dad say, "Okay, girls, you've had your fun. Give me those cans, plant your feet fight here, and count to twenty." They were scared shitless, so they did as they were told.

In those twenty seconds, Rockwell got his towel back, covered himself, and was handed the cans of string-fetti. His dad opened the shower door again and let Rockwell blast the girls to his heart's content. They went crying like babies and left the area. That soothed Rockwell's ruffled feathers a little, and he and his dad had a good laugh over it.

Dinner that night was as requested earlier—lobster and steamers for two and fried chicken for one. Retelling the shower story to Russell was hilarious. Even Rockwell could see the humor in it now. Russell was so sorry he wasn't there to see it all happen. He said, "Where did the girls go? They really couldn't tell anyone. They started it. They'd be in deep shit if their dads knew what they were doing. About how old were they? Hey, Rockwell, they must have a thing for ya"

Russell couldn't let it go. He thought this was the best thing since white bread, but the last remark got under Rockwell's skin, so he jumped out of his seat and emptied his large cold iced tea over Russell's head and said, "It's your turn for a shower. Let's see if they come back!"

Their dad just watched his two boys with merriment in his heart, a beer in his hands, and thankfulness that this dining area was outside!

"Okay, guys, we have the motel for tonight and tomorrow night. Check-out time is eleven a.m., so on Thursday, we hit the road again. We'll be heading home south through Massachusetts, stopping and stretching our legs at Old Sturbridge Village. I think you'll enjoy seeing some old history and experiencing the way they worked and lived back in colonial days. We have to do at least one educational thing this week, but I think that will be a fun one. I've been there a couple of times myself and think it's just the thing for this trip. But for tonight, how about that arcade we saw when we drove in?" their dad finished.

"I know Russell's dying to get over there," said Rockwell. "He's envious of the King of Kong system Hamm has at his house. They spend a lot of time playing there."

The first thing Russell did, before even stepping into the place, was take a picture. Just inside, he took another to show the enormity of the place. *Now this is going to be fun*, he thought. He was beyond excited! *Wait until I show Hamm this place!*

It got dark and late so fast. They were having so much fun, and they didn't want the night to end, but this was not a twenty-four seven establishment. So at midnight, the lights blinked. That was the invitation for everyone to leave.

Once back at the motel, they took their shoes off and draped their jeans over the back of a chair. The bed was such a welcome sight.

All the sleepy travelers slept until nearly nine the next morning and awoke ravenous. Rockwell was already up and in the outdoor shower, with the door locked. He decided that this was the one thing he'd love to bring home, or maybe build one at home. Dreaming aside, it was time to eat...again!

This time, the three of them walked the entire length of the famous Hampton Beach boardwalk. They took a right and went one block back to a neighborhood Breakfast Kitchen, so the sign in the window said. As much as two young boys could be charmed, out came their cameras.

This day was filled with water slides, not the ocean (it was too cold), and roller skating. By the time they got back to the motel, sprawling on the bed and watching TV was all the excitement they could muster for the time being. All the traveling and constant activities had caught up to them. Exhaustion hit, and it was an early night.

Wednesday/Thursday

"We'll be staying in a motel one more night and traveling the rest of the way home on Saturday," their dad said at breakfast on Thursday morning, back at the Breakfast Kitchen.

The boys were sorry to leave this fun place. They promised themselves they would come back again someday, but the next place they were going was only about an hour's ride away, so off they went.

When they traveled like this, it was hard to find and keep a radio station for much more than three or four songs before static cut in or they'd lose the station completely, so there was really nothing to do but to talk with one another. So talk they did, all about their best friends at home, Hamm and Kevin, and about what they were going to tell them about this trip. Dad was chipper as well, listening and asking questions and generally showing a lot of interest.

Before they knew it, they were pulling into the Old Sturbridge Village parking area, but there had been a water leak the day before, and the village was closed until further notice.

From out here, the boys couldn't see what they could be missing on the inside of the village, so their disappoint was minimal.

Now back on the road, the boys could tell their dad was racking his brain for an activity that was rather close. Traveling Route 20 was a real drag. He knew that the state of Massachusetts was working on a toll road in this area. How he wished it were open now. Thinking out loud, he now had to explain what a toll road was and how they collected money to use it.

After traveling a bit, still on Route 20, they passed through little town after little town. Each town had a grocery store, an eight-room school building, and a post office. Finally, when they entered Auburn, there was something different…a movie house. Having been disappointed with Sturbridge Village not being open, they pulled into this parking lot, read the marquee for the movie, and decided to try it out. The feature this week, the whole week, was Disney's *Treasure Island*.

The boys had never been to a movie theater before, and they knew of the Disney movie, so their excitement once again peaked. Dad was glad he could save the day with the movie. But when they entered the building, they were assaulted with popcorn butter nasal overload. He said, "No, no, you can't have any. It's still morning. Enjoy the movie. We'll do lunch later." They couldn't be too disappointed. Breakfast had been just an hour ago!

The movie was great. They were back in the car and on the road again. They couldn't stop talking about it. Excitement like this pleased their dad to no end. Every once in a while, they'd mention that this was the fourth little town they'd driven through since the movie.

"Hey, Dad, do you know where we are going?"

Their dad always looked relaxed and comfortable no matter where he was. *I guess that comes with being an Army man*, Russel was thinking. And then there it was—a sturdy-looking shack boasting "Ma's long dogs and soft buns." It was just this little hot dog stand on the side of the road.

"How would you know this was here?" Rockwell asked, looking around in bewilderment. "What a neat place. We don't have anything like this at home."

"New England is a quaint and welcoming place. They have a lot of little treasures like this dotting the landscape from Maine down through Maryland, Connecticut, and Rhode Island. I hope you get to travel it more as you grow up. Don't eat too much here. Dessert isn't too far away, just a short drive."

"So you do know where we are and where we are going!" said Russell with his mouth full.

After downing a couple foot long hot dogs, they were back in the car again. There really wasn't too much to hold their interest in riding around again. There was a post office, school building, and a big factory. That was different. There was a coffee shop, a gas station, and a church. It was much like the other small towns they had driven through, until they turned right and headed up a hill. Their dad took a sharp left and stopped abruptly, parking under trees.

"This is an apple orchard, boys. Get out and smell the sweet aroma and eat a few. You can fill those bags from Harry's and bring them home."

Once again, they were amazed. They had only seen apples from the grocery store or fruit stand at home, never anything like this. After climbing a few trees, throwing apples at one another, and filling their two Harry's bags, Dad did hurry them along.

"Hurry, get to the car. We have to get out of here."

He heard voices coming from up the hill. It seemed people were walking their way, and he didn't want to get caught parked off the road and taking two bags full of apples. Rockwell took his time getting back to the car. Then he retrieved his camera to photograph this marvelous place.

Dad lost his patience and yelled, "Get in the car now! I said we're leaving."

Rockwell was stunned and did what he was told. It was the first time all week his dad raised this voice and had shown displeasure with him.

When leaving the orchard, Reginald had the overwhelming urge to head up the hill. They drove, slowing past a few houses and a cow field. Rockwell enjoyed seeing the cows and smelling the real earthy smell of the land. The last house was at the top of the hill on the left and looked rather new for the area, and then there was just more cow field. Without his dad knowing it, Russel took a couple more pictures.

It was a quiet ride for a while until Rockwell said, "Sorry, Dad. I just wanted to take a picture of the orchard with us in it, but it's okay. I have that picture in my head."

With the silence broken, the ride was once again comfortable. Their dad announced, "New York City, here we come." He continued, "It's about a three- or four-hour ride from here." They groaned from the back seat. "We'll find a hotel room for the night. Then in the morning, we are going to the Statue of Liberty." That brought rounds of cheer and discussion about a hotel. They hadn't done that before. The next three and a half hours were very quiet ones for their dad. The boys had fallen asleep.

Friday

The traffic in New York City was like something out of a movie. Rockwell and Russell's reaction was silent excitement and full attention. Again, they wondered, "Dad, how do you know where to go?"

The hotel they pulled into boasted an indoor swimming pool, taxi service to the airport, and daily buses to the Statue of Liberty. Excitement overflow started to occur at the enormity of everything around them. The New Yorker Hotel boasted about their forty-one floors. Once checked in, they took the elevator to the thirty-first floor. It was a quiet ride up. Dad thought the boys were holding their breath!

Now it was nervous excitement that overtook both boys as they looked out the windows and whistled at how high up they were. Their excitement led to thank-yous and thankfulness overboard for the past week and "what should we do next?" wonderings. Dad supplied two options. "The pool closes at eight p.m., so you have time for that, or we could just eat…again!"

All the apples were dumped into the wheel well in the trunk of the car so the boys had their Harry bags for their clothes again. They pulled on their bathing suits. Dad even joined them, and they headed down to the ninth floor and the pool. Rockwell was full of questions as to how they could have a pool on the ninth floor with people in rooms under them. Russell, with his twelve-year-old intelligence, went into a lengthy explanation of this phenomenon. (Ya gotta love 'em.)

The pool room was dimly lit, had deck chairs on three walls of the area, and a wall of glass highlighting the New York streetscape below. The pool itself was lighted about one foot deep to illuminate the turquoise swirls in the pool walls. There was an elegance added to the space by the hanging light fixtures lit so low, and matching fixtures on the walls also turned to very dim. The swim rejuvenated all three of them and built an appetite.

Over dinner in the dining room (one of three at this hotel), their dad reviewed the next day. "Once again, check-out time is eleven a.m., but we'll be leaving before that. I think we can manage breakfast, move the car to the ferry area, and be on our way to the SOL by eleven. That will give us three or four hours on Ellis Island to explore and learn and head home by three thirty or four to get there around dinnertime. Can you see? All plans are made around eating!"

Upon reentering their room on the thirty-first floor, Dad was handed an envelope from the main desk that contained a key and a note that read "Room 3108, 11:00 p.m." Reginald's knees went weak, the palms of his hands sweaty, and his penis was erect. All things not to be ignored.

He said, "Busy day tomorrow. Straight to bed." With that, there was no arguing. To bed they went. Reginald sat on the edge of his bed and pondered Crystal's intentions for showing up here. He'd only mentioned in passing the Statue of Liberty as a maybe, but he knew that she knew this hotel in New York would be the chosen one. They had enjoyed many nights here over the years.

It was not a time to question her intentions. He taped up the note and got down there. He'd get laid and get back here to get some sleep. He was exhausted!

He knocked on room 3108. Then he opened the door. Crystal was a beautiful women with shoulder-length hair the color of sunshine. She had eyes he always got lost in, breasts that were begging to be sucked, a tiny waist, and legs that started at the blond pussy. They were already in the air on pillows, just waiting for him.

"You're right on time," she crooned.

"I didn't expect to find you here," he said as he was kicking off his boat shoes and unbuttoning his shirt.

"You never know when or where I am going to show up, now, do you, dear?" she whispered in his ear as he lowered his naked self to her mouth to ravenously kiss her until his tongue was so tied with hers that his penis almost started without the main course. He moved his mouth to the left breast and nipped eagerly at her taut high nipples. His right hand cupped her pussy and kneaded the extremely swollen little clitoris with his index figure.

"I know why you came here tonight. You needed this. You are becoming a whoremonger. Sometimes you can't get enough of me. Just when you think there is a situation I can't get away from, you show up with the hottest, horniest thoughts and feelings. Haven't you learned that's when I excel?" Reginald almost felt as sex starved as she was exhibiting. He was reacting to her summoned calls with zealousness.

With that, he spread her legs, dipped his head, tongued her sexy lower lips, and sucked her clitoris. He inserted two then three figures and drove her to the heights she longed for. Before he let her ecstasy escape her, he filled her mouth with his tongue and filled her sex box with his longing, throbbing manhood. He pushed, and she rose up and pushed back. They had a rhythm that worked, and he held that orgasm for a very long time. With both of them spent, she gave him permission to leave.

Once back in his own room, on the thirty-first floor, alone in his own bed, thoughts of Crystal and never doing this again started entering his head. She had become very needy and very demanding. He could handle the sex and keep up with her sexually. It was turning up in these personal places that was starting to bother him. Never before had she insinuated herself in his family. He didn't like it. But that was her endgame. She'd run to Rhonda if he failed to comply with her wishes.

For a long time, it was fun. He realized she fed his fetish and fulfilled his fantasies. But it had to end. He had done something this week he never consciously thought he would. And then having her show up…his worlds could collide.

"You'd better grab a couple of apples to have on the island. The juice and coffee cake won't last too long in your stomach once we get moving!" their dad yelled back at them before they left the car. They were standing on the dock, waiting for the ferry. They were glad they grabbed their jackets, not just for the pockets to hold the apples but because standing near the water was a little chilly. Every move they made was a new experience. Talking to the other people on the dock and people watching had become a thing. Reginald panicked when he saw the familiar Italian silk wrap around Crystal's beautiful hair. She was standing not ten feet from them. How dare she.

They took the ferry to Ellis Island, walked through the halls so many foreigners and refugees had walked through, climbed the stairs inside the statue, stood on the island, and looked back at the skyline of New York City. Everything in that afternoon was exhilarating and exhausting. By now, both boys had taken all their pictures. Their counter was at twenty-five. Hopefully, they'd get twenty-five pictures from the roll. Someone would need to help them get the mailers filled out and then send it out for processing. Their dad said that was how it was done.

"Don't worry about it. I'll take care of it for you," he said.

The ride home was short for the boys. They slept. They never knew about the side trips their dad made in the night while they slept. They never knew about his trips around the sun when he paid them to be busy!

The Bedroom

It was after dinner when they drove into the driveway back in Towson, but the minute they stopped and the car shut off, they were up. Home and up.

They raced one another into the house. They couldn't wait to tell their mom all about their adventures, but in doing so, they disturbed the twins and woke Riley. The only one happy to see them was Rachel. Once she got off her mind that she was a little tiffed that they got to go away with Dad but not her, her two older brothers had her full attention. So while the two boys ate a bowl of cereal, they told Rachel all about fishing and swimming in the ocean, swimming in an indoor swimming pool, about the cookouts, about the arcade, the ferry ride, the hot dog stand, the apple orchard, the thirty-first floor, and the Statue of Liberty. Every now and then, they would take a breath, take a bite, and start their story again. Rachel was completely enthralled with their tales and got caught up in their excitement.

Mom was quieting the twins, and while she was doing so, Dad walked the floor, holding Riley and listening to the boys entertain Rachel with their enthusiasm.

It didn't take long for the house to settle into the normal family hum with the twins in bed, the three older ones getting ready for bed, and their mom and dad with Riley in the bedroom behind closed doors.

Rhonda was so happy to have Reginald behind this door with her again. Usually, his homecomings were her time to be with him. She was totally taken off guard when he arrived home last week and immediately took off with the boys. So now it was her turn to take off, which she did. First went her blouse, then her bra, never taking her eyes off of him. She pushed her shorts and panties down to the floor, stepped out of them, went closer to him, and wrapped her naked body around his now aroused, fully clothed one. His hands couldn't work fast enough to touch, caress, unbutton, unzip, press, and finally kiss! Her hands helped to unbutton, pull down, pull off, wrap around, and massage the unit she wanted and waited for, for a full week. She groaned and leaned into him, never releasing her hold on his penis. Now she bent to wrap more than her hand around his prize. She tongued the wet tip first then hungrily pushed her mouth down hard on him until his pubic hair tickled her cheeks. Again, a groan of delight at having him pinned to her in a most delightful way escaped her full mouth. Coming up just a little and letting his penis rub the inside of her mouth, she whispered, "Welcome home."

"If only Cry…Christ…if I'd known that waited for me, I could have been home two days ago. Every woman should know how to do that."

"You've let me practice over and over. I'm glad you enjoy one of the things I do best. Now for the next."

She began the process of straddling him, with his penis reaching, stretched high into the air, begging for attention. One more little nibble and she impaled herself along his entire length. This time, it was he who groaned.

"I've practiced that as well," she bragged, but he abruptly turned in a way to knock her off, and he sat up.

"I'm not having you pregnant again!" he spat. But she calmly pressed his shoulders back down onto the bed and began the magic with her tongue on his now wilted manhood. He was so easy. It didn't take long, and the promise of birth control in use brought about the swift change she was hoping for. She'd see the boys in the morning.

The morning came too soon for Rhonda. Having Reginald all to herself for this one night wasn't enough. He had robbed her of a week of companionship and good sex. Damn, he was good! But for now, they had a houseful of kids that needed their attention.

Rachel was already up and eating a bowl of cereal in front of the TV, with Ruby and Rose laying on the floor, watching as well. Rhonda joined them, holding Riley after he'd been changed and fed in the kitchen. Within minutes, Russell and Rockwell joined them. Now the room was getting a little noisy. Rachel didn't want to hear about their adventures again. Ruby and Rose didn't know what adventures were, and their mom's attention was anywhere but on her boys.

"You can tell me about that later, okay, guys?" She was leaving the room, holding Riley with one arm and stroking Rockwell's hair with her other hand. She was doing it ever so gently as she walked past them, going back into her room.

"No matter," Rockwell said. "I'm off to find Kevin. I know he's never been to Hampton Beach. He'll want to know all about the slides and the arcade."

Russell was a second behind Rockwell and said he was gonna go and find Hamm and tell him all about it too.

With that, their mom told the twins to each eat a banana, and she closed the door to her room. Reginald was sitting on the side of the bed, just ready to head down to the bathroom with a promise he'd be right back. Having heard Rhonda give the twins instructions to have a banana, he handed them each one on his way back to the bedroom.

Rhonda wasted no time getting Riley back into his crib then stripping down and getting ready to receive Reginald from behind, doggy style. These were the mornings she was made for, craved, and performed best in. The kids were busy and wouldn't bother them for a while. So when Reginald got back to the room, she was center in the bed, on all fours, and purring, "Do it this way first."

Without additional preamble, Reginald, ready and rock-hard, gently at first, and then with more force, had Rhonda filled and rocking to near screams of delight. But with past practice in this houseful of children, Rhonda was ready with her boy toy, soft to the touch but hard enough to bite on, stuffed in her mouth to absorb her groans and throaty cries of ecstasy. He imagined what Rhonda looked like mouthing and fucking and groaning with a fake penis sliding in and out of her wet delicious mouth. He grew harder and more anxious to have that sensation on his penis. So with practiced maneuvers, Rhonda was now filled with tongue, fingers, and a slowly sliding and ever so expertly placed store-bought penis. While he was making his move to fill her with ways to completely undo her control, she had his balls in her hands and his penis halfway down her throat, just the way they both liked it. He was settled into this posture of pleasure, stroking Rhonda's legs and reaching up to her breasts, wanting to fill his mouth with hard little nipples. He readjusted his body to first kiss the inside of the mouth that had so sweetly teased his prick to release and then lowered his mouth to be filled with the left then the right breast. They filled his mouth to perfection. The two of them just lay there, enjoying touching or being touched. That was what had started for them nearly thirteen years ago.

Reginald Sabers

Rhonda had just arrived in New York City with her folks who were fine jewels and diamond brokers for a firm in Roanoke, Virginia. They so wanted her to follow in their footsteps, having taught her and had her schooled in metallurgy and cutting of precious stones. But lately, she couldn't concentrate on the tasks at hand or the business her folks were leading her toward. Her father, of Austrian descent, was strict with lessons and learning proper etiquette and obedience. While her mother, a tiny beauty from the back streets of France, was as quiet as a mouse and obedient to a fault. Poor Rhonda didn't stand a chance at individuality or personal growth of any kind. So when the opportunity presented itself that day when getting off the train in New York for her to have coffee—proper afternoon coffee in public with a man in uniform—her dad didn't refuse on her behalf because of the preceding circumstances.

It was such a chance meeting. So many people were crowding the train terminal. Passengers were coming and going, all in a hurry. They were carrying suitcases, duffel bags, paper bags, and business portfolios, trying to get through the exits and entrances all at once. Lovers were holding on to one another, and parents were clutching onto children's hands, and hundreds of military personnel were trying to get to the proper track as to not miss their train back to their bases.

Marie Tuffin was bumped from behind. She lost her footing and fell to the ground. The rolled felt sample sack of rough-cut diamonds was knocked out of her hands and half unrolled at the feet of many travelers. The scramble to help Marie back on her feet and secure the felt roll was helped along by a handsome officer in uniform, who noticed the felt first and the daughter second. In unison, all four people moved safely out of the building and huddled together in a more private spot, where the bundle was inspected by the jeweler.

The jeweler offered his hand to the officer, saying, "Oliver Tuffin. My wife, Marie, and our daughter, Rhonda. We thank you most profusely for your quick thinking and assistance with Mrs. Tuffin."

"Ahhh, Sabers. US Army at your service, sir." The officer returned the handshake with his own introduction.

"Are you headed back to base soon, Lieutenant Sabers?" asked Mr. Tuffin, who addressed him by name and rank because he recognized the stripes on his shirt.

"Shortly, sir. But first, I have some business at the New Yorker Hotel on Madison. But until then, I have some personal time and would like to spend that time with your daughter over coffee, if you would allow me."

Rhonda just looked from her father to Lieutenant Sabers with hope in her heart. Once her smile broke out and they promised to meet them back at the jewelry store by five, her mother spoke the permission.

In an instant, Lieutenant Sabers offered his arm and walked Rhonda away from her folks and down the street to an outside cafe.

Rhonda, with her inners all a flutter, had just fallen in love.

They had one cup of coffee and a conversation that never ceased between the two of them. Five o'clock came too soon for both of them. When he stood up to walk her back to *Callini Jewelers*, she faced him and said, "You never told me your name."

Right there on the sidewalk, he took her in his arms, looked down into her eyes, and said, "Rhonda." He was drawing it out, as only he could do. "Such a lovely name. Reginald…I'm Reginald Sabers, and I feel that I was just born because of you." With reluctance, he stepped away from her. He offered his arm again, and they walked in silence.

When they were standing together outside the jewelry store, Reginald reached inside his shirt pocket, reread the note, and swore softly that these were orders, orders at this moment he wished he didn't need to follow. But it was crystal clear, he needed to!

"When I have finished my business, may I see you again? I know we've just met, but there is so much more to you that I want to get to know better. Am I too presumptuous to invite you to dinner tomorrow night at the hotel? I can pick you up or meet you there. Where are you staying?"

Rhonda's heart leaped with joy at the invitation, but she did not know how to answer. She had family obligations and work at the store. Feeling so conflicted, she promised to meet him at his hotel at 6:30 p.m. tomorrow. She'd find a way around her folks.

That night at the chateau, where they always stayed when in New York, Rhonda barely ate any supper. She fidgeted with her clothes for tomorrow like she never had in the past and wished her hair was a different color and would behave in a style more becoming a young woman than a child. Sleep was nonexistent for her tonight. Her mind was filled with thoughts of Reginald sitting straight in an outdoor chair, Reginald looking deep into her eyes, Reginald holding her hands across a cafe table. Reginald, so handsome in his uniform. Reginald, waiting for her at his hotel.

The next day dragged for Rhonda. She worked side by side with her mother, telling and retelling her coffee time with Reginald the day before. Marie was not a stupid woman. all the signs of her losing her little girl were beginning to show. In her heart, she wished her beautiful daughter all the love and freedom in the world—everything she felt she didn't have. Oliver was a gentle and considerate lover, but all of his considerations ended when he walked out of the bedroom. Social appearances and obedience from his subordinates (wife and daughter) and employees were paramount. He was not to be made the fool by anyone! This was the world of Marie. She hoped for so much more for her daughter.

"Go see your young man," Marie finally said when Rhonda, having no appetite for lunch and watching the clock all afternoon, just paced behind the necklace counter, arranging and straightening already straight chains and lockets. Rhonda's face brightened, and she froze in place at her mother's words.

"Really, Mom, you'll cover for me with Father? He'll put you to task for allowing me this pleasure. We both know what he is like."

Marie just butterfly kissed Rhonda's cheeks, slipped a few coins into her pocket, and watched her walk away.

It took Rhonda fifteen minutes to walk the distance between the store and the New Yorker Hotel. At first, she wasn't noticing any of her surroundings. But just then, she liked the feeling of the sun, now low in the sky, on her face. Yesterday, Reginald said it brought out the sparkle of her golden light brown eyes and the beautiful rusty highlights in her hair. The breeze was blowing her rusty-colored hair into her face and eyes, but his description of her only made her feel mysterious and feisty this afternoon. Not being under the thumb of her father also made her feel that way. Thinking of Reginald waiting for her made her inners flutter again. And then she was there. She saw him standing under the awning of the front doors, and her breath caught in her throat.

He walked to her, took both of her hands in his, kissed her lightly on one cheek, turned, and walked her into the most elaborate dining room she had ever seen. He could tell that she was a little nervous but also delighted to be there. He asked her how she got away from her folks and was able to meet him. This broke the ice, and she started talking.

"Mom actually gave me permission to come and see you. Said she'd soften Father's feathers if need be. So I am freely here to be with you. I've been looking forward to seeing you again all day. I almost didn't recognize you without your uniform. Have you been waiting long?" She took a breath to keep talking, but he stilled her by reaching for her hands again across the table.

"My uniform is not who I am. And yes, I think I have been waiting for you...all my life. I also had a long day thinking about you and that haphazard head of rusty hair that only you can pull off. You look wonderful."

She self-consciously touched her hair and admitted to him that she hated the color and everything about it.

They ordered and ate dinner. Easy conversation followed that they forget they had just met. Their conversation touched on everything. His family, mom and dad, were deceased by a train crash nine years ago in 1930. He was an only child growing up near the army base in Roanoke, Virginia. It made it an easy enlistment for him the day he turned eighteen, five years ago, well after WWI. He told her of some of his travels overseas and within the United States.

He said, "Growing up the way I did and losing my folks at a very formidable age, I think I was always an adult and never really a kid. I've always taken my responsibilities very seriously right down to the way I handle money. The service doesn't pay a lot, but it houses and feeds me. And for the most part, it supplies most of my clothing, so for an evening such as this, I can wear my own clothes, eat, and pay for the food I want. I can sit at a table with the person I want. It is so nice to be able to choose." He continued, "And I choose you. You entice and capture my interest like no one else ever has. You have filled my every thought since we've met."

With that, a waitress appeared with the dessert menu and awaited additional orders, breaking the spell that had just fell upon them. When the waitress walked away, Rhonda got back on the subject of getting to know him and parents.

She told him that she had a very open relationship with her mom, much to her father's astonishment, because such matters shouldn't be discussed with children.

"He is such a pompous ass sometimes. Mother has admitted to me that he knows her menstrual cycle down to the day and has planned his sexual exploits accordingly to plant no seed and produce no more babies." Rhonda's face was now showing indignation for his superiority. She also leaned in a little closer to Reginald and lowered her voice a bit. "Mom also beams at the fact that she knows she is his only lover because when her monthly cycle is safe, that first bedding when intercourse is now safe, he enjoys bringing her to such sexual heights that his release is supercharged. Mom has alluded to other sexual methods, but she said I'd have to explore those and find out about that for myself. She said control in the bedroom can and will be one of my greatest pleasures if I find the right man." All this time, Rhonda's hair was slightly swaying as she turned her head and bobbed back and forth for emphasis. At this, he couldn't not fall in love.

When she realized that she had monopolized the conversation with such personal insights, her forehead and cheeks turned pink. She hadn't realized that during this whole time, she was dreamily looking into his eyes, holding his hands, and rubbing his fingers. She was drawing circles around his palm and wrists and just being herself.

Reginald was so glad when dessert arrived. The table above his lap and the table legs between them saved him from reaching out and exploring what Rhonda had under the table, under her shirt, just inches from his hands. Rhonda hadn't noticed how labored his breathing had become or how disinterested he was in his dessert. His total interest now was on Rhonda's mouth and how she delicately placed the spoon on her tongue and licked the chocolate sauce from its little bowl. While it was still in her mouth, she turned it and licked the underside. All of this undid Reginald's equilibrium. It was happening while Rhonda was still talking about growing up under her father's thumb. It was a good thing she was still talking because he couldn't stand up if he wanted to. His penis was doing all of his standing!

With dessert consumed and the bill for dinner taken care of, Reginald escorted Rhonda to the sidewalk outside, where it was considerably cooler, thank goodness. It was now time to walk her home and get back to the hotel to carry out his other orders. Being a lifer in the military was once his career goal, but now he wasn't so sure. Before he took his leave of Rhonda, he was assured of seeing her again tomorrow—same time, same place. But he told her it was the last time because he needed to get back to base in Maryland.

Rhonda entered the living room of the little chateau her folks had rented at a respectable hour after being escorted home by a young man, but was that good enough for her father.? She approached her father and kissed his cheeks, as was her normal good night ritual, before starting to turn toward her room.

"Don't you leave this room until I say you can leave this room," he barked.

She was half turned and hated to turn back to see his dark angry face, which was already ingrained in her brain, but turn she did.

"Yes, Father?" she whispered in his direction.

"You are not to see that military man again. He is too old for you and too worldly in his manner. Is that understood?"

Rhonda just looked at him with hurt and almost hatred in her eyes and heart. "Yes, Father, I heard you. But see him again…I will. Please don't make me choose between the men I want in my life."

Now Oliver was on his feet and in Rhonda's face. "Defy me and I shall never talk to you again."

Marie was in the doorway with tears in her eyes, witnessing the exchange between her two loves.

Rhonda stormed from the room, past her mother, to her own room. She'd gotten a taste of freedom and even love tonight. She craved more. That night, she tossed and turned, but two faces flashed before her eyes each time she tried to close them to sleep—her father with daggers in his eyes and Reginald with merriment in his.

The next day passed in silence between Rhonda's parents, Rhonda and her father, and worst of all, between Rhonda and her mom. She thought, *This is no way to live. I'll let no one run my life but me.* So at the end of the day, she walked home, packed a bag, left a note taped to the ice box door, and left the chateau for the last time.

With her small valise, she once again walked to the New Yorker Hotel, where once again Reginald was waiting for her under the awning at the front doors. This time, his greeting was amorous, including a full bear hug and a kiss full on the lips. With weak knees, she felt very at home in his arms. When he released her, he noticed a difference in her immediately. She was no longer shy or standoffish at all but rather self-assured and confident.

This time, she took his hand and said, "If we only have this one night left, I want us to make the best of it. No holds barred. And when it is over, no regrets." Without another look back, they proceeded to the elevator and exited on the thirty-fourth floor and entered room 3412.

Reginald took the lead now and put her valise on the nearby stand. He was still looking at her straight in the eyes. She never wavered or looked away from him. She just stood there and started to unbutton her long dark dress. Her fingers moved slowly and deliberately on each small pearl button while keeping her eyes glued to his. He was spellbound by her movements as the dress started to separate and expose a nakedness he'd not expected at this juncture of disrobing.

Rhonda had stripped naked at home and just slipped this long dress over her body. She did not want to falter once she started her advances toward Reginald, and she didn't want to give him a chance to change his mind. He let her continue with her slow movements of disrobing and started to unbutton his own shirt, each of them keeping complete eye contact while trying to control their breathing and outward composure. This was definitely a first for Reginald, to be stripteased by a woman without even being touched. He was so turned on. He knew he loved this wild-haired woman. He continued to disrobe but faltered and just stared at the lovely sight in front of him.

Reginald started toward Rhonda to speed the process, but she held him back with a look of animalistic dominance and personal space. Without even finishing the process of unbuttoning, Rhonda pushed one shoulder free, then the next, and let the dress fall to the floor to expose her perfect feminine physique. Reginald, still silent and tongue-tied, looked but didn't touch at the beautiful body in front of him being bathed by the late day sun streaming in the large street view window. The sun was bathing the red and rusty highlights of the long tendrils flowing over her shoulders and down her back, and his eyes fell on the rusty triangle patch before noticing how long her legs were. He'd never seen such beauty. He only felt nakedness in the dark.

These were new firsts for him today, as Rhonda's naked body approached him and finished disrobing him, one garment at a time. She still wouldn't let him touch as she bent to push his trousers and boxers to the floor and witness, for the first time in her life, a fully aroused naked penis. Thrills went through her body as were witnessed by the nubs growing on her perfect (he judged) mouth-sized breasts.

Still without either of them speaking a word, he took her by the hand and placed her perfect body against his and kissed her slowly. At first, the touch of his naked body pressed against hers was a little startling. Then add the kiss and she was over the moon and enthralled. The kiss deepened when he felt her returning the kiss. It became all-consuming with mouths opening to allow more probing, eager tongues finding pleasure spots.

Sunlight was still streaming through the large windows, high-lighting the center of the bed. He never met a female more relaxed in her own nudity and exposed herself so willingly.

"Rhonda," he said with a croak in his voice. The silence broken. "I want you more than I've ever wanted anything before. You've done that to me in such a short period. I'm yours for the taking. May I take you and make you mine?"

The honesty she heard in those spoken words was so unexpected that she cried. He was so undone by her reaction. He pulled her close and held her and caressed her and slowly rubbed her back. He fondled and twisted her hair until the tears stopped.

"I've never been wanted like that before. I just walked out of my parents lives to be with you. It was my choice, and you validated me in such a loving way. I'm yours. You can take me any way you want." She returned his words.

The sun was setting on two bodies entwined together in kisses and love. The gentleness with which Reginald took her made her believe in fairy tales and Prince Charming. His hands were everywhere on her body, stroking, rubbing, and probing. Her wetness guaranteed easy access without much trouble. Once he had her soothed by his touches on her arms and neck, love bites and suckling on her breast, kisses down her stomach and licking her behind the knees, she knew no place on her body was off-limits to his touch or his exploration.

This was a totally new experience for Reginald. He'd never had a virgin. A virgin in every way. One to cherish, handle with kit gloves, and teach. He needed to cram into this one night a fortnight's worth of loving, because he would leave at noon tomorrow. Rhonda's willingness to bend or sit or stand or reach for the sky lent itself to all new feelings and ways of giving, and she took so well. It was all so intoxicating and thrilling. She loved being touched.

So when she reached for his manhood that stilled him. She fondled and came close to his ear and whispered, "I want you to drive your penis into me and kiss me at the same time. I want your body to probe and fill me everywhere at once. I want to feel you when you're doing it please. The first time should be special. We have one night, one night to hold in our memories until we can see each other again and renew these feelings."

"I don't want to hurt you. The first time can be very uncomfortable—" She wouldn't let him finish.

"So get it over with so we can do it again and enjoy it," she said between clenched teeth.

At that, he unclenched her teeth with a deep probing kiss and penetrated her for the first time. Her arms came up around his neck, her legs came up around his waist, and her tongue licked back at him with such desire that he came before she could pump back at him twice.

One night with Rhonda was not going to be enough. Her technique at clenching his penis tight in her pussy was something he'd never experienced before. Her verbal exploits of his body were also new to him, and he learned that he loved to hear his name on her lips when he drove her to new loving heights.

With her, there was no second or third time. Each time was like the first…new and exciting. They excelled together.

The morning came too soon. One more time would never be enough for them. But up they must get. He loved her naked body. She strode across the room with no inhibitions and showed him all of her.

Loving in the shower was also the greatest.

She slid soapy hands across his back, around his chest, and down to his cock. She played to her heart's content until the twinge between her legs said, "My turn." She wiggled in front of him, bent, and let him enter her from behind. Nothing was off-limits. They had no limits and a lifetime to learn more.

He was dressed in uniform again and returning the room keys to check out. She asked him, "When will I see you again with you returning to base?" It was a thought that was also on his mind. "Where is the base?"

He held her hand and walked her to the same cafe where they had their first date. Just when their coffee arrived, so did Rhonda's father. She saw him and started to rise from her seat. He slapped her across the face and said, "I disown you. I will never see you again."

Reginald was out of his seat and on his tail so fast, but Rhonda stopped him and said, "I knew that was coming. Let him go. Remember, my choice was to be with you!"

"Finish your coffee. We have something we need to do before noon," Reginald stated flatly.

Rhonda was a little shaken by her father's appearance and needed the coffee and a minute to recuperate. When Reginald's words sunk in, she asked, "What do we need to do? Where are we going?"

Now Reginald's face and tone of voice had changed, and he announced with whimsical amusement in his voice that he was going to make an honest woman out of her and marry her, here and now if she would have him.

The whole morning crowd at the cafe heard his announcement and cheered her on with instructions and directions to the courthouse.

By 11:15 a.m., they were married. At 11:30 a.m., she had her bus ticket to Fort George G. Meade in Maryland and instructions where to meet him on base at five that afternoon. At noon, they each boarded their separate buses, going to the same place.

At 5:00 p.m. in Fort George G. Meade, Maryland, the bus terminal was very busy, greeting many incoming buses from many different locations on the east coast with disembarking patrons of all color, sex, and rank. Among those arriving were Reginald Sabers, Rhonda Sabers, and CC Clear. They were all on different buses.

The Horrible Summer

"Mom, Dad…help! Kevin just fell out of the tree camp. His leg looks awful. It's going in the wrong direction. Hurry, help! Rachel, go get Mr. Schaffer."

So much for a sexy homecoming, Rhonda thought. *Boys will be boys*. Up they got. They dressed in a hurry and met Jerry Schaffer, Kevin's father, in the backyard under the willow tree. The poor kid was laying on his back with his left leg under him pointing toward his head, definitely going in the wrong direction. Kevin was just sobbing and sobbing, not even trying to be macho. His pain was very evident.

While Mr. Schaffer and Reginald were strapping Kevin into the back of the station wagon to transport him to the hospital, Rockwell was explaining to his mom that they were up in the camp talking about the vacation and all the fun they had in all the places they stopped. Just then, they were talking about the movie *Treasure Island* his dad brought them to see, making believe the camp was the island and stretching forward to see land. Kevin fell out!

It was a long three hours waiting for the doctors to fix Kevin up. Rockwell had never been in a hospital before, and after today, he never wanted to again. But truth be known, this was just the beginning of a long road that Kevin and, at times, Rockwell were going to travel together.

The remainder of that summer was really the pits for the two boys. Rockwell stayed by Kevin's side playing board games and cards, and they sat and read their summer reading books. Rockwell would think back and recount the shopping trip before their romp from one motel to another on their vacation when his dad bought him his books to read. He was glad now. A trip to the library to get books would be lonely because Kevin couldn't join him. Kevin couldn't do anything. He couldn't put any weight on his leg. Even crutches were off-limits for the first three weeks. Then only around the house, not even outside.

Now it had been six weeks, and school would start the next week. Rockwell was told he was going to school, but that was still off-limits for Kevin. The leg pained him quite a lot, and the swelling hadn't gone down as the doctors had hoped. Surgery was still needed to pin the bone in place to hopefully help it mend back in its proper position.

So on Monday, Rockwell headed off to school. He was in fifth grade now. Kevin and his mom headed back to the hospital for more x-rays and hopefully schedule the surgery that would enable Kevin some mobility.

At three thirty, right off the school bus, Rockwell was at Kevin's door to find out how they made out at the hospital. He hoped better than he made out in teacher assignments. He got Mrs. Heartburn… Mrs. Heartbryn…the witch!

"So how'd you do? When is surgery, and then when will you be able to walk again?" Rockwell streamed all his questions together as Mrs. Schaffer set out milk and cookies.

It was explained that Kevin would be operated on in mid-October if—a big *if*—more swelling went down. Then there would be a soft cast until the stickers came out, maybe two weeks. Then there would be a removable hard cast. With cast off, he could bathe. With cast on, he could maybe walk with crutches. It was still going to take some time. She said Kevin understood that there would be no school for him until maybe after Christmas break. In the meantime, he was going to need a tutor.

"Lucky Kevin. I got Mrs. Heartbryn. But I'll still come over every day after school. We can do our homework together. Besides, I still need your help with math. Learn it real good with your tutor so you can teach it to me. It's a two-for-one deal."

Kevin didn't let his leg get him down. Schoolwork kept him busy. Rockwell was true to his word and came every day, and TV was getting better. Kevin's dad even let him have comic books, which was a no-no last summer, but they were still censored, and Russell wasn't allowed to sneak any of his in. Russell's were a bit too mature and did not feature the proper Wonder Woman for Mr. Schaffer's taste for Kevin's level of learning.

October came, and the leg was operated on with only minimal success in that there was more damage that they hadn't originally known. That explained the pain element that still plagued Kevin. Over the next eighteen months, Kevin's maneuverability only advanced to 100 percent with the use of crutches. They went everywhere he went. He was given a stick to ward off jokers, wise guys, bigger kids, and pain in the asses. Its striking power was ruthless and powerful.

The leg on a ten-year-old boy was not done growing, so the fix that was done that day in October nearly two years ago was just the first one. Two years later, at age twelve, Kevin's leg needed to be medically rebroken and set with pins and rods to support his body, hopefully for life.

This actually was an exciting prospect for Kevin and his family because success in this operation meant no more crutches and the ability to walk and run under his own power. It was explained that this was not going to happen overnight. But with physical therapy, exercise, and time, the leg could almost be normal again. Once again, they started the pre-surgery appointments of x-rays, blood matching in case they needed blood during the procedure, and height and weight measuring for the proper implants. This time, these appointments didn't bother Kevin but rather gave him hope for an unencumbered future.

This was a day Mr. and Mrs. Schaffer, Rockwell, and the Sabers would never forget. Rather than proceeding with the repair on Kevin's leg, the surgical team exposed a large mass of cancer starting in Kevin's upper thigh continuing into the bone and bone fragments surrounding the original break. This unexpected turn of events changed everything. The doctors immediately closed up the initial incision and needed to discuss this discovery with Kevin and the family. Breaking this kind of news to an almost teenager and his family was hard. It was heartbreaking to everyone. However, with its discovery, immediate actions needed to be taken to ensure it did not spread and infect more areas.

Over the next several months, Kevin was poked and prodded. Tests were run, and blood was taken. Several specialists were consulted, and over time, a plan was in the works. A new procedure of stem cell transfusion had been known to work in many types of cancer. Finding the proper donor was the first important step, and the second was trials to make sure the donor's cell would not be rejected. This procedure had been known to be time-consuming and, in some cases, painful to both patients.

The decision to try this procedure was made, and the donor search started. They didn't need to look far or long because Rockwell insisted he be tested. He came back a perfect match. The Sabers' decision to allow Rockwell to be the guinea pig for Kevin was an easy one. They went for it. Healing one boy ensured the other would be whole again. Rockwell suffered nightmares and terrible bouts of depression over Kevin's injury and being an almost invalid for the last couple of years.

The summer of the boys' fourteenth year saw such improvement in both of them. Kevin's parents couldn't be happier with the success of the bone cell procedure, and Rockwell's parents swelled with pride over their son's endurance through the entire experience.

The healing process was immediate in Kevin's body and just as immediate in Rockwell's demeanor with regard to dreaming about tomorrows.

Life went on, and life got better for the two boys. They were now normal teenagers, still sharing experiences, girls, stolen cigarettes, hitchhiking into the city without anyone knowing, barhopping while underage…yeah, normal and finally fun!

High school graduation was just a huge party week, and then they were off to New York to find an apartment before school started again. They were going to be freshmen together at Rensselaer Polytechnic Institute and room together for the next four years. Rockwell was an excellent student, and Kevin was a chick magnet. So when they shared their talents, both boys always had dates and, most of the time, great grades. Having an apartment off campus didn't hurt either. Every once in a while, the refrigerator needed filling, or the car needed gas, so they went to Samaritan Hospital to sell blood. They could go there every six weeks. As time went on, they learned to also go to Albany Memorial Hospital and sell more as long as they were diligent about where they went and how often, not to mix up their visits to the hospitals. St. Peter's Hospital and Ellis Hospital were also added to their source of income. Every now and then, mostly when they returned to school after a holiday break and the folks were generous with cash, they would go to the hospitals to donate blood. There was always a disaster of some sort, and it was needed. This kept them in good graces at the various hospitals. They learned more than reading and arithmetic at school!

14 Years Later

Auntie Lynn and Uncle Chuck had just celebrated their tenth-year wedding anniversary, and Maddie was babysitting little Jamie and Todd when she called home to her mom for help. Maddie developed a terrible headache and needed help immediately. Sooner, if Mom could manage it. Andi drove as fast as she could across town to Lynn's beautifully landscaped, lighted, and carefully appointed brand-new garrison. Lynn deserved all the happiness and better things in life that came her way. She and Chuck worked hard for all they had and appreciated all that Andi had invested in their friendship. Every chance she got, Andi would make sure the pool they were looking at was installed properly, or the boys' Little League team or T-ball had proper T-shirts and up-to-date equipment. Andi learned generosity from her mom and was grateful she had the funds to share.

Poor Maddie. All from a headache, and the next five months would be hell in diagnosing and settling on the proper method of treatment of chordoma. This is a kind of cancer that grew in the base of your skull and spine, most likely by cells left behind at childbirth. It was very rare. Only one out of every one million got it. Only about three hundred people were diagnosed with chordoma in the United States each year.

This unwanted visitor at the base of Maddie's cranium grew to the size of a thumbnail and was just starting to press on vital neurological spine endings. Stopping it's growth and removal or shrinking the growth was vital to Maddie's having free movement in her limbs and normal bodily functions in the future. Having done her due diligence as a doctor and Maddie's mother, Andi was hoping that the stem cell insurgence, a fairly reliable procedure, could work. This was the way the oncology department and doctors wanted to go. All things depended on finding a matching donor for further stem cell testing to fight this insidious cancer. Blood samples from Maddie were needed to type her blood and search for the right match in a donor. There was no father on record or other family members from his side of the family to try to match her, so the search was tough and with no results. All townspeople knew of Andi and Maddie's plight and struggles and turned out in droves to try and help with the donor matching. Still to no avail.

Again, there were no family members left in Andi's family tree, so the cry for help went out to neighboring towns. And again, the response was phenomenal.

With all testing done, there were two anomalies that kept reoccurring in two individuals that needed closer checking into. A holiday blood drive in Troy, New York, in January 1964 had produced the name of R. Sabers, indicating seven of the ten strains of likeness. It indicated a family tie. A letter was penned as a personal plea from Andrea to the hospital and Red Cross regarding this name and their blood drive of January 1964, reaching out on any long shots for her daughter. This was so long ago. It would be on a wing and a prayer if they got a return call. Second, there was a sample from a Ms. Dora Samson, no address listed, which was collected during a donor drive that was specifically for Maddie five months ago. These results had an 87 percent field range, which could be promising for a match.

All the posters of plea and request for blood sampling that were plastered on the walls of the hospital cafeteria and parking garages and family and friends' waiting areas were now replaced with posters of "Please help us to identify Dora Samson. No information other than resident of Worcester County, using this facility listed on her 'permission to draw blood' documents. She helped and may be our angel in this search. If you know Dora, please reach out to me at: VE9-4581."

During lunch with Andi one day, at least five months after the testing, Pat, a colleague of Andi's at UMass Medical, remembered her receptionist had taken a long weekend a number of months ago to attend the wedding of her favorite neighbor, a gal named Dora. Shortly after that ceremony, Sally, the receptionist, gave notice on her job to move to Arizona to accompany her friend and new husband for Dora's husband's medical issues.

Hope sprang eternal in Pat because of her esteem and respect for Andrea, so on a hunch, Pat reached out to Sally to ask her friend if she had given blood in Worcester for helping a thirteen-year-old girl who needed a procedure to help cure her cancer.

The call led to much confusion in Pat's heart, coming from her friend Sally's repeated reply from Dora. Dora responded with babbling about her thinking Arizona was far enough away that if anything came of the blood sample, she would not be found. Pat was dumbfounded. To first reach out in a life-and-death quest and then refuse to or seem to refuse to step forward because your initial kindness paid off. This wasn't right. Something was wrong.

Pat's head was spinning. *What to do? Who to talk to? Can there be a long-distance transfer of Dora's blood to here? If need be, can the names be withheld if that is the problem?*

With these questions in mind, Pat went to Andi with her vague information on Dora and posed the same questions.

Andi listened but only half heard once the donor seemed out of reach. She had it explained to her again. Andi's mind started working like a criminologist, not a mother.

"Let's go back to the initial application and see what or how she listed her name and family members." Within hours, Andi had the application with the names, dates, and locations. She held the paper with shaking hands as she read the names and locations and dates on the application.

"It can't be," she muttered. "The family line ended with Mom."

Pat said, "What are you talking about? What family? Whose mom?"

Just to make sure she had it right in her head, Andi started a family tree with her grandfather, Martin Samson, and Judith at the top. "Grampa born 1900, Judith Wright Samson born 1902. Their only daughter, Amy Samson Chambers, born 1927. Aaron, Andrea 1946, etc. 1949 to 1964. Maddie…here we are…the end. There is no Dora," Andi said.

With another look at the application, they saw Dora listed as being born in 1918, making her sixty-three now, in Roanoke, Virginia. That location…Virginia…all of it sat funny in Andrea's psyche. Her father's name was left blank, as was her mother's. Andi remembered her mom saying she met her dad in Virginia. Coincidence? Time was running. She tried to make a connection where there was none…but what kind of connection?

"I'm taking a trip," Andi said. "It's high time I take a vacation. I've never been to Arizona."

Lynn was always happy to hear from Andi, but with this news, it startled her. "Yes, of course, Maddie can stay here with us. The boys will love it. When do you leave?"

"I got a flight out of Boston tomorrow afternoon at four, getting into Arizona at four thirty their time. Weird, ha!"

"Well, happy hunting. I sure hope you find what you're looking for. I hope you're not setting yourself up for more heartbreak with this woman."

"Please don't tell Maddie why I've taken off like this. Please cover for me. She worries more for me than for herself." With that, Andi packed a suitcase for a week. She called Matt Driscol, her supervisor at control, and informed him of her snap decision for this trip and started dinner.

Maddie was excited to be staying with Aunt Lynn and the boys. She was also glad her mom was getting away for a while, even though she knew most of the trip was for work. Andi and Maddie talked a lot about Andi's work, her job at the Criminal Behavior Unit on the twelfth floor at UMass Hospital. They had lengthy discussions about how the mind worked in relationship to criminal actions and how the brain reacted to many different stimuli or situations, i.e., drugs, sleep, lack of sleep, sex, starvation, temperature variations, birth order, or any other anomaly occurring in the patient's brain. Andi was proud of Maddie and her level of understanding, both of her own health situation and the working of the world in regard to medical, social, and political protocols. Being brought up by a single mom and being subjected to all the hearsay of Andi's past, discussions between Lynn and Chuck, and snips from Lynn's parents, Maddie was a pretty grounded kid.

Since Maddie was in the fourth grade, and one of her friends' mom was getting a divorce, she started asking questions about men or, more profoundly, about dads. Did she have one? Where was he? What was his name? What color hair did he have? Was he tall? Did he have a mustache like Cary's dad? These questions always put a giant smile on Andi's face, and she answered in her most honest and loving (and evasive) way.

That she, Maddie, was a miracle child, made in such a beautiful place by the most handsome of all men. "Just picture your Prince Charming," she would say. "And wrap him in coats full of honor and honesty, gentleness and kindness. That's your dad, because you are all of those things."

To date, that worked, but someday…

* * *

Arizona was hot and unwelcoming. It was too hot for May. Her hotel room at the Layette Regency in downtown Caltoken was clean but too near the ice machine, and she soon leaned on a shared wall with a groom-to-be, living it up and partying with three other buddies before his nuptials. Her rent-a-car was not ready upon her arrival, and when delivered, it had little to no air-conditioning. This was why she didn't travel, she mused, as she waited for another car to be delivered. As a token of apology, Keepers Rental offered her comped dinner at the hotel dining room until she could travel about. She was starved, so that was the first good thing to happen to her.

Dinner was more than adequate. She was delightfully surprised by its presentation and quality. Going out for dinner was one of Andi's highlights as long as she got what she paid for. This was most divine and excellent. As she was signing her slip and leaving a generous tip, leaving her room number, the hotel manager wandered over. He already checked her out. She checked in alone, had *Dr.* attached to her name, and was gorgeous. Not very often all the right qualities came wrapped in one package. He hoped in the next week, he'd have an opportunity to unwrap a bit of this package and get better acquainted.

"Good evening, Dr. Chambers. I hope you enjoyed your dinner. Can I interest you in a brandy or coffee with Baileys to finish it off? Excuse me for being so forward. I'm David Messier, the hotel manager, and I'd like to make sure that so far, all things are to your liking."

She thought very quickly, loving the idea of coffee with Baileys. She invited him to sit. "Yes, please, the coffee with Baileys sounds wonderful."

Once he sat, Andi went into her critiquing the meal she had just devoured. It was an A-plus delight to the pallet, and she looked forward to the coffee as a finisher. However, to make her stay an even better arrangement, not sharing a wall with four young men out to sow wild oats, getting drunk, and manhandling the ice machine would be greatly appreciated. Could he do anything about that?

"You do say what is on your mind," he said to her, still brandishing his best smile.

"Of course, and I generally get what I want. I know how to ask, how to pay, and how to say no. So when my business is concluded,

I'd like to send you a thank you note and go home and rave about your establishment and my stay."

The coffee arrived just as his smile started to waver, but he managed the save with "I'll check at the desk as soon as we've finished our coffee and make sure we can get you more suitable accommodations."

Lynn would have skinned her alive for her abominable behavior just now, but she felt drooled over and rated on a scale of one to ten just as she always was by men who thought they were in high places. But she got a new room.

Once she was settled into her new room, Andi called Maddie. Maddie sounded so happy and content just being at Lynn's and promised she'd take her meds as prescribed and on time. Although this sounded like a practiced response to any mother's concerned request, Maddie knew a life-threatening thing was happening to her body. And all things considered, taking a few pills a few times a day and blood testing at the hospital once a week, although a pain in the ass, very necessary.

While talking with Maddie, Andi relaxed and let the strain of the day and having coffee with Mr. Messier drain away from her. Maddie was her life, and the longer they were on the phone, just talking nonsense, the more relaxed Andi got. Now she took in the soft colors of yellow and gold in the wallpaper and darker yellows and greens in the still life paintings on the wall. She was sprawled across a queen-size bed with a gold brocade bedspread and matching pull drapes across two sliding glass doors to an inviting patio. With her eyes, she followed the light green carpeting into that which she knew was the bathroom.

"Good night, sweet girl. I miss you already. A shower is next, and then early to bed for me. Kiss Lynn for me. See you in a few days Love ya…bye."

With that, Maddie said, "Love ya" back, and they hung up.

Friends and a Coke

While she and Lynn were building a home for themselves and the baby, and transferring Lynn's scholarships and entrance papers to Worcester State so she could stay close to home for Andi, the war in Vietnam raged on. Jake didn't fare too well in the draft lottery and left for the Army in January of 1965. By then, Andi hadn't seen him but maybe twice since the concert. One time he visited in the hospital, and one time they bumped into one another at the post office. She remembered leaving the post office that day, thinking, *Yes he is too handsome for his own good, but why do my knees still buckle at the sight of him? My arms want to circle his neck and pull him close to me. Why does my heart still skip a beat whenever that kiss crosses my mind?*

Too much water under the bridge for thinking anything could be between them. That was a long time ago.

With a hint of a smile, Andi also remembered Tom being really crushed when Lynn broke up with him to date other guys at school. The smile was because Lynn's Chuck was Tom's older brother who always said Tom was not good enough for her.

Thirteen years later, they were still finding cash and valuable holdings in her dad's name. The memories flooded back. The attorneys were Baker and Comstock with George Comstock her appointed executor. She didn't know she had attorneys and bankers and insurance in the beginning, Andi felt guilty taking any money out of the account her attorney had set up for her. She needed to, of course, for her own living comforts and to help Lynn with school. She couldn't believe how much money she was spending on the baby's needs. The hospital bills and upcoming hospital bills were taken care of by the attorneys from her accounts. This was a necessary evil, and she was made to understand that these amounts of money did not dent the balance in the accounts. That was a good thing to know and to hear, but one of these days, she needed to know how much money and how many accounts were in her name and how much money she was paying out to Baker and Comstock for their assistance. She didn't lose sleep over these things anymore. George was a good guy, and when she was ready, Andrea contacted him, made the proper appointment, and met with him at his office and was educated in the manner of money...her money. She had seen the ledgers before but didn't understand a thing she was looking at. George made it simple for her:

Account number 227, Madeline Samson from husband's life insurance,1940: $941,016.00

Account number 1043 balance of Nobel Prize Award: $1,789,441.00

Account number 2678, Martin Samson life insurance: $401,012.00

Account number 6954, Higgins & Platen (Martin Samson's former employer still using his inventions): $4,011,006.00

"All of these balances are, as of three thirty yesterday afternoon, you understand, a total of $7,142,475.00."

Andi saw the number but really could not comprehend the enormity of it. She said, "George, please say out loud what that number is."

His smile said as much as his next few words did. "Seven million, one hundred forty-two thousand, four hundred and seventy-five dollars. Like I said, that was at three thirty yesterday. Those numbers have grown today."

Andi remembered sitting there with her heart pounding and her vision blurring as she tried again to look at the ledgers.

"Oh yes," George said. "I forgot the slush fund that you draw from weekly to run your house. That balance is one million, seventy-one thousand, three hundred seventy-one dollars." He wrote it down for Andi to look at: $1,071,371.00. "This is the account that is funded at a rate of 15 percent annually from the other accounts I mentioned. That is the annual stipend available to you. Our fee has also been paid from this account as you don't drain it, and it makes for easier accounting on your year-end taxes. Our fee is ten percent of the balance in this account on January 15, before it is refunded for the New Year. Our amount runs around $3,785.00 a year."

For some reason, Andi trusted George and knew she had enough money for her lifetime. Once she cleared her head of what the numbers looked like, she went home, told Lynn she had enough money for life, and shared a bottle of Diet Coke. They never spoke of it again.

Money

Andi smiled to herself. She was feeling proud of the fact that she had instructed George to set up gifting accounts—nameless, of course—to Mr. and Mrs. Marsden in the amount of $50,000 annually, with the same amount to Lynn and Chuck and also the same amount to each of their boys annually. She started this the year Lynn's first son was born. That was six years ago. Since her first meeting with George, her slush fund, as George had called it, drained every year. Lynn's education was not cheap. Her education was through-the-roof expensive. Chuck's start-up funding for his solar company was handled. Her little house, off the beaten path, was exactly what she had dreamed of, but she always thought it out of reach. Every penny spent for other people was handled with the utmost secrecy. Lynn and Chuck never knew. Andi never told Lynn how much money she had.

Baker and Comstock's annual billing also increased with Andi requesting these different accounts be implemented.

She was thinking now, *I've not thought about money this much in a long time. I wonder if Dad has gotten any richer in the last year or so? The last windfall came from a hidden metal box dug up two feet from the mess hall on the grounds of the Navy base in Virginia. I've learned that*

Dad was a crafty soul, always up to something. Note to self, call George and establish scholarship funds in Dad's and Grampa's name. Yeah… that would be a good thing.

Dora

Feeling utterly exhausted now, she hoped she could shut off her brain, get some sleep, and contact Dora in the morning, sharp and ready.

The next morning, Andi got up the nerve to call Dora Samson Williams to arrange a meeting. At first, Dora was startled to learn that Dr. Andrea Chambers was in Caltoken. But during the call, after the reminder of the blood test and subsequent follow-up documents, she realized this lady was the child's mother.

"Yes, of course, Dr. Chambers. Please come along. we are about forty minutes from your location at the hotel. Please come for lunch."

That's all it took. Andi dressed in a cool-looking two-piece pant-suit of light blue. She grabbed a straw handbag with matching straw open-toe sandals, pearl earnings, sunglasses, and a water bottle. She was off. So far, the day was mildly warm and sunny, just like her mood so far. On her way down to the parking garage, she eyed David Messier behind the desk. With a quick flick of her glasses as a gesture of hello, she scurried to the elevator before he could make a move toward her. This car was nicer. It was a tan Chevy Malabo with air-conditioning that worked. Once on the road, Andi found a radio station that was easy to listen to and thought about the upcoming interview.

* * *

That telephone call set Dora to pacing. She told her husband, Richard, that Dr. Chambers was coming for lunch and for more information about the blood donor form from Massachusetts. He looked at Dora with concern and reminded her about the connection of DNA markers in her blood that were similar to the girl with the problem.

"You say that the girl's mother is this Dr. Chambers, and she is here. That tells me that she has more to talk to you about than she just let on to you."

Dora starting pacing again. "Richard, you are the best thing that has ever happened to me. You know that!" She looked at him with eyes filled with love and longing. "I'm sixty-three years old, and you make me feel seventeen. I've waited for you all these years. I don't want you to hear what you are about to hear, because I know she is going to ask the right questions to scare you away or for you to mistrust me. I've been through the ringer myself with some of these realizations and fact-finding missions. This poor gal has no idea what I'm about to tell her."

Richard sat down, a little dumbfounded at that winded statement Dora made. "Sit down with me," he said. "Fill me in a little before she arrives. But no matter what, I love you and would never be scared away. We are good together, and that's how we are going to stay…together."

Dora sat next to Richard, took his hands in hers, and started. "Dr. Andrea Chambers is my niece, but she doesn't know it." Before the entire statement was out of her mouth, Sally entered the room with a look of shocked understanding at Dora's words and her hesitance toward helping.

Richard looked at Sally and said, "You knew this?"

"Not really, Richard. But a few weeks ago we…Dora got a call from Pat at the hospital. Remember Pat, my friend? She relayed the blood numbers to us and asked if Dora…" At this, Dora began to cry. Sally stopped talking because it was not her story to tell anymore.

Richard stroked Dora's arm in comfort and offered her his handkerchief. Those tears had more to tell, but he was willing to wait. Dora was a beautiful woman who had carried a lot of burden all her life, and it was all about to come off her shoulders.

Sally offered to make lunch, telling Richard she was glad Dr. Chambers was here and that her recollection of Dr. Chambers was one of kindness and patience. She told Richard that Andrea Chambers was a young and very good-looking woman with very striking and sad green eyes. Now it hit her. *Oh my god…they were Dora's eyes.* They were probably sad because she saw a future where she lost her only daughter.

Dora and Richard sat in their very sunny well-appointed family room. On a glass wall hung bamboo-like drapes. It had light tan carpeting under stuffed chairs and assorted couches and tables, all with lamps and vases full of flowers of every color of the rainbow. The lovely room, however, did nothing to relax Dora's feeling of dread.

With no preamble, Dora started with "I had never talked about my life or fears when I was a kid or all the empty searches or longings to belong or be really loved by…anyone. When I discovered a name, one of notoriety, I became scared and didn't know where to go with the information. After all, I was only a girl working in the library at the Naval yard in Roanoke, Virginia. Who would listen to me and help me open doors and talk to people in the know about abandoned and abused children? I couldn't drag the name of a great scholar through the mud, so I sat on my information and intuition until it started to give me ulcers." She rattled all of this out without any expression at all.

Richard, still holding her hands, sat dumbfounded. But he now understood why she would never talk of her childhood. He felt sorry for the little girl he never knew.

Dora stiffened her back, looked straight into Richard's eyes, tugged on both of his hands, and announced to him, "I am the former Dora Samson, born in 1918, unwanted, unloved, abandoned, and left-for-dead daughter of the Nobel Prize winner of 1927! But more than that, I am your wife, and I feel more love and respect than I knew existed in this world."

All the emotions expressed in those words brought them both to tears and into an embrace that only love could build.

Sally was in the kitchen, dicing and chopping celery and onions and chicken for salad, and she heard most of the conversation. Dry eyes were not to be had anywhere in that house. Once Sally composed herself, she brought iced tea into the sunroom and deposited the tall glasses and pitcher within reach of Dora, who was still sitting on the couch. Sally bent at the waist, hugged Dora, and told her Dr. Chambers was going to love her.

Within minutes of Dora's verbal exposé, the doorbell rang, and lives were about to change.

Dora gave Richard's hands a final squeeze with her best smile spreading across her face. She rose from her place to answer the door. She gave herself a second for a final deep breath and swung open the door to welcome her visitor.

"Dr. Chambers, welcome. Please do come in. We've been waiting for you." With that, Dora walked Andi into the room and introduced Richard.

"My husband, Richard. And I'm sure you remember Sally from the hospital back in Massachusetts. Please have a seat. Iced tea has just been provided by her thoughtful hands."

Andi couldn't take her eyes off Dora. She self-consciously slipped into the room, staring at and becoming tongue-tied at the sight of Dora. Never having been a shy person or a woman of few words, Andi just wanted to engage Dora in conversation face-to-face. But then…she stared into the mirror image of her own eyes. The overwhelming feelings of familiarity embarrassed her to the point of apologies as she tried to relax.

"Dora, you have a lovely home. Thank you for allowing me to visit with my errands and personal matters to discuss." Andi uttered those simple words almost in a whisper.

Dora caught the look on Andrea's face when she walked in. She was also caught a little off guard. She looked into eyes so green and familiar, flecked with white, almost like neon. She had so many emotions all at once, so many truths to disclose, years of facts to uncover, so much to lose or gain. They were two people with a bridge to cross to find those truths.

"Dr. Chambers, please let me take the donkey by the tail and get to the point of your visit. I realized just a bit ago that the youngster in need of this blood is your daughter, and I might be able to help."

"Dora, it's Andrea or Andi, please. And yes, she is my daughter. Maddie is my only child, the reason I get out of bed every day, the little person who taught me to love. I'd go to the ends of the earth for that little girl. So you see, that's why I'm here." Andi took a deep breath, reached out to take both of Dora's hands in her own, and added, "Please, won't you help us?"

With an audible gasp, Dora looked straight into Andi's eyes and said, "I still have that donkey by the tail, so I'm going to take him out on a limb and ask you to call me Aunt Dora. Andrea, you are my niece. That's why my blood type could be the saving grace for Maddie. We have a lot to talk about, and I have so much to tell you."

The room stood still. Richard was the first to make a move. He was in awe of his wife who disclosed, for the first time in her life, a bit about her background, and that was just a few minutes ago. Now she was willing and wanting to tell all, her life story, to this virtual stranger sitting here, holding her hands.

Richard held up an empty glass and cheered, "Hear, hear. Drinks all around while we get to know one another!"

That was enough to break the spell in the room. Slowly, smiles began to show on all the shaken faces looking at one another.

Sally poured the iced tea and began the conversation, going back to Worcester when they were doing the blood drives. It took through lunch and all afternoon to get to the part where Dora admitted running away to Arizona with Richard to avoid being found in case her blood was needed.

"I had been so lonely. So when Richard popped the question and suggested this move, I was all in. I could run away from my past again with the love of my life and live happily ever after. I'll admit, I forgot all about Worcester until that call a few weeks ago." Dora scanned the room, but her eyes fell on Richard, and she said, "I'm so sorry for using you and not letting you into my past and deepest fears. I let you take me away, so I hid again. You made me happier than I've ever been, and I thank you, but now it is time to face my past and live up to my responsibility."

Richard jumped to his feet, reached out for Dora, and embraced her with love in his eyes. "Darling, use me any time you want. Whatever you need to do, we'll do together. Next, we get to meet our great-niece."

"Speaking about great-niece, let's back up a bit and lay the factual foundation as to why you are or think you are my aunt," Andi said, looking straight into Dora's unmistakable eyes and lost her heart before she even heard the undeniable facts about Dora's life.

While they sat and talked for hours, moving from the sunroom to the dining room for lunch and the lanai for afternoon snacks and more iced tea, Dora once again revealed her lifeline, growing up in foster homes and orphanages and group homes. All these experiences hardened her and made her a good listener. That's why once she worked at the library in Virginia, she was able to piece together her lineage with everything but a proper birth certificate. Having made peace with her findings, belief that her silence on who her father was, was the proper course of action because he and his wife were already dead. It was time to move on with her life and not dwell on the could have beens.

"But now, all these years later, here we are with undeniable proof that we are family, because it all comes down to blood."

Dinner that evening was a barbecue of huge proportions, prepared by Sally and Richard with the conversation now in all directions. Andi was so sorry she had no pictures or mementos of her mother. They were all lost in the fire. All of Dora's longings to have something tangible or learn more about her half sister or father were gone. Now the conversation was turned to Andrea's past and family and education.

No, they had never apprehended the man who raped her. No, they had never apprehended the person who set the fire at her family home. And no, she had never married. But one odd fact still needed to be investigated, and that was there was one more blood sample with possible family traits.

"Dora, yours is not the only one!"

After a pleasant dessert, plans were made to meet back in Worcester at the UMass Medical Center in two weeks. Andi started the drive back to her yellow room at the Layette Regency. The drive back to the hotel was uneventful and even a bit peaceful after the last several hours she had just spent with "family." Boy, what an odd concept for her after all these years. She had an aunt. She wondered if her mom knew of her half sister. But no, Dora said she made no inroads to meet any family members or make any contact at all.

For a change, it was wonderful to talk about Aaron and his friends and how tall he always seemed to her. How he would tease her about anything and make her crazy happy to spend time with him and his older friends. Alley and Alex were so real in her memories. It warmed her heart to be able to remember their endless chatter in their own language, always seeming to have a secret the way twins generally do. Adam was just coming into his own, playing big brother to baby Abby while she was still struggling with potty training. Oh, the memories, sweet and always heartbreaking at the same time. Andi was happy and willing to share and talk about the family she lost that lifetime ago with Dora. It was a pleasure to bring up the past and fill Dora with stories of past birthday parties or Christmases filled with warmth and love all because her mom and dad were there. That sort of love and merriment was lost on Dora because there was none of that in her past, but she was eager to learn and to hear all the tales Andi could relate to her, especially those remembrances of her mom.

Andi spoke of her mom with such reverence that Dora couldn't get enough. Amy was nine years younger than Dora, born into a family of a loving mom and dad. When Amy spoke of her childhood, it was always the fun stuff she'd bring up, like the way her dad would make learning fun and interesting. Andi admitted she didn't know a great deal about her grandparents because they died so many years before she was born. The only thing that she remembered her mom saying to her over and over again was that he, her dad, had the most beautiful eyes and, she (Amy) was so glad two of her children had inherited that family trait from him. That made Andi remember one other thing she'd have to tell Dora someday. One of the twins, Alex, had the same green eyes where Alley did not. For the first year of their lives, that was how they could tell them apart when they were sitting next to each other. Oh, she hadn't thought about that in such a long time.

"Thanks, Aunt Dora. That was a great memory!" she said out loud.

Pulling into the parking garage at the hotel, Andi realized how much she needed this day—everything she had learned and everything she talked about. How easy and fun it was to remember her mom and dad and brothers and sisters, and most of all, she was getting the help her daughter most desperately needed. She was smiling from ear to ear as she walked through the lobby of the hotel toward the elevators. She was lost in her own thoughts, enjoying the peaceful feeling she had. Andi didn't see David heading her way to once again start a conversation, to bother her, to hit on her.

"Hello, beautiful. Did you have a good day? You look radiant with your cheeks smiling and your eyes all lit up."

This time, Andi didn't hesitate to accept the friendly gesture and returned his smile with her own. "Yes, had a great day, a very fruitful and informative one at that. Thanks for asking. Right now, I'm off to call my daughter and share some good news and then early to bed. Thanks for the comfortable stay. I'm leaving early in the morning, catching the six a.m. flight home."

With that as her final word to David, the elevator doors opened, and she disappeared within.

Donor Found

The flight back to Boston was uneventful, which made it a good flight. Leaving her car at the airport was a good move on her part as well, which made getting out of Boston and back to the Worcester area faster without having to bother anyone for a ride. Lynn was always her backup plan, but she was glad she didn't need one. Spring in New England was beautiful. Everything was new and clean again. Today, the air was fresh and a cool sixty degrees with only a slight breeze. How nice she could think about the weather and appreciate the clear blue sky and be happy. She was heading home with some good news and what she prayed would be the miraculous end results to Maddie's suffering. She was happy. She hadn't felt this way in a long time. She should have been nicer to David Messier.

Lynn was in the backyard enjoying the sunshine and reading a book when Andi arrived. It was perfectly evident to Lynn that Andi was very pleased with her current mood, and she couldn't wait to hear the details of her trip.

"Oh, Lynn, this was such a terrifying and wonderful and fruitful trip. Where is Maddie? I need to tell her too," Andi said breathlessly.

"I talked with her last night briefly, but only about the people I'd met, not about the good news. I wanted to tell you guys together. I'm so excited!"

"Okay, girlfriend, breathe. I can tell you're excited. Maddie has the boys down at the park with their big wheels. Make the noise down there, I say, better than here…right?"

Lynn was getting up and directing Andi toward the house, now talking about getting some lunch ready.

"Come on up. While we make lunch, tell me all about Arizona. You sure left town in a hurry the other day. That's not like you. Maddie was hoping you met a guy and were following him to a resort for a lover's holiday. She thought that would be wonderful for you."

"Oh…she did!"

"Even when she told me of your phone conversations and the excitement in your voice, you couldn't dissuade her of that notion. She's gonna be happy to see you, but sorry there's no guy in your life…is there? Terrifying and wonderful in the same sentence says guy to me. No wonder why she thinks so," Lynn said.

"Be real. You know I went in search for a blood donor for Maddie. I found one."

At that, Maddie came bouncing into the kitchen, wrapped her arms around her mother's waist, and made her repeat that last sentence.

"Glad you're home, Mom. Now repeat that last sentence for me." Maddie looked up at her mother with tears in her eyes and disbelief in her young heart.

Andi saw tears running down her daughter's cheeks, and it was her undoing. The excitement she had been feeling for the past forty-eight hours and having her daughter wrapped around her brought on her own rush of tears.

"I found your donor, sweetheart, in the most unlikely of people, at the most timely of times in our lives. It's a long and wonderful story. Let's make lunch. I'll tell you when we sit down." She continued to hug and hold on to Maddie.

Lynn, standing at the counter, looking at and listening to two of the most incredible people in her life, couldn't hold back the tears either. Just then, Jamie and Todd came running in and stopped abruptly and stared at everyone crying. Not understanding all the tears, they each grabbed one of their mother's legs and started crying along with the females in the room.

"This is a sad turn of events," Lynn said as she squatted down eye to eye with her boys. "These are happy tears, guys. We don't know exactly why yet, but Auntie Andi will tell us over lunch, so go wash up."

This ended the tear fest, and lunch was prepared in haste.

In between bites, Andi tried to relay all her new information of Aunt Dora and Sally and reviewed the blood screening done in the greater Worcester area months back, all to get to this point of having a viable donor for Maddie.

"Arizona was hot, very hot. Everything was air-conditioned. Dora and Richard's home was lovely and comfortable with a sweeping view into the desert through their wall of glass in their sitting room. The house was about forty minutes from the hotel I stayed at, which gave me time to think while driving both ways."

The boys grew tired of grown-up talk and wandered away to play.

Andi continued, "My thoughts were completely different driving in those different directions. My first ride was filled with trepidation as to what this woman's feelings were going to be at meeting with me. The ride later in that same day was a new me, anxious to get back here to you and share all the news. So back to Dora…I guess my grandfather was quite the randy back in his youthful days. Love 'em and leave 'em…but I really can't believe he could have been such a cad as to leave a girl or woman pregnant and alone. Dora's life as a child was sad and lonely. She was love starved and parentless. She learned to make her own way in life but wanted desperately to find and build some roots, so her paternal search began. If I had met her any time in her past, I would have known her and not questioned her parentage. The minute she opened the door to welcome me into her home, her eyes spoke to me. You'll see when you meet her. She has my eyes! And now in the autumn of her years, she has found Richard, the love she has been searching for forever. You should have seen them. They are so good together. I am so happy for her, because now she's got me…us." She looked at Maddie for confirmation.

"Aunt…Dora," Maddie said, dragging it out. "Not a boyfriend for you. I'm almost sorry for you, Mom. But really excited for me. So can you explain what we need to do and when for the procedure."

With that, Andi patiently started to explain, with a few details, what would happen next. Lynn and Maddie were riveted.

"First, I need to put a team together to meet with Dora, Aunt Dora, in two weeks. That is the time line we've set up to proceed with your procedure, Maddie. Hopefully, all systems will be a go after her first go-around with the high doses of chemo that are needed for about a week or two prior. This can be a tough process, because some donors had been known to get side effects like nausea and mouth sores and headaches, and they were younger than Aunt Dora."

At this point, Maddie reached for Andi's hand for motherly support and doctor reassurance. Andi held her hand tight and continued, "When the high-dose chemo is done, then we can start the transplant. The new stem cells are given to you through an IV. Neither one of you will feel any pain from this, and you can be awake while it's happening. After the transplant, it could take two to six weeks for the stem cells to multiply and start making new blood cells. During this time, you'll will be in and out of the hospital and then making daily trips to the hospital to get checked by the transplant team. It can take six months to a year until the number of normal blood cells in your body gets back to what they should be."

At this, Andi turned her full attention to Maddie and said, "Honey, this is the miracle we've been praying for." With that, Maddie tried to leave the table, but Andi added, "You do know even with all this going on, you are still going to school, young lady."

Maddie smiled brightly and bolted from the room.

Lynn and Andi stayed where they were for a few more minutes in total silence.

"So how was she while I was gone? Were the headaches really bad?"

Lynn tried to be a little evasive, but Andi knew the score.

Later that afternoon, Andi checked in at her office at the hospital to make sure there were no fires to put out or problems to solve. Fires to put out…such a strange and eerie passage to convey a problem and bring up old memories. They were memories better left unremembered!

Andi loved her daughter to the moon and back and would have loved the chance to love Jake back in the day, but that didn't happen, and she'd been too busy to have a guy in her life, the way Maddie had put it. So why was she thinking of that now? She still wasn't ready. She still had a few personal fires to put out.

Why, after all this time, was she thinking about the two maybe blood matches for Maddie? As it turned out, Dora was a gold mine—a relative and donor, all wrapped in this wonderful person. She'd investigate the other sample and name in a few weeks. "Let's get through one major hurdle first."

With all her fingers crossed, she got on the phone and called a meeting of surgical, oncology, and blood technicians that were going to be needed to perform miracles for her daughter. This was stressful enough when she was dealing with someone else's daughter, but doing it for her own tightened her stomach and made her head throb and her eyes water. Professional or not…this was personal!

The last time she needed to pull together a surgical team of this magnitude was for Alan Pierce in Walpole State Prison. She was the only one Alan would talk to and confide in. Way back in what seemed like another lifetime ago, Andi remembered Dr. Gayle Hampshire having a positive effect on her and her choice of studies, majors, and subsequent choice of career. If she could do for just one person in this world what Dr. Gayle had done for her, her mental suffering could count for something. At the time, Alan was it. This time, it was for her as much as her daughter.

Introductions

Two weeks flew by. Andi was so busy at the hospital. She was getting together all she needed for Maddie's big day. When she got the call that Dora and Richard had arrived, she was ecstatic and relieved. Somewhere down deep in her subconsciousness, she was afraid Dora would chicken out and not come. That was the mother side of her, letting the fear show. The doctor side pushed those thoughts away.

Dora and Richard had flown into the small Worcester airport. They rented a car and settled into the Driftwood Motel not too far away before Andi had a chance to check on them. The Driftwood was a favorite restaurant/motel combination that Andi had recommended several times to colleagues over the years, and she knew Richard would be comfortable there while Dora was in the hospital. But tonight, they were coming home with her. Andi couldn't wait to introduce Maddie to her aunt Dora.

Andi had bought her little dream house on Robin's Nest Road a few years back and still enjoyed it immensely. It was just perfect for entertaining guests like tonight in the dining room. It sat eight comfortably but felt cozy for her party of four tonight. Its dreamy chef's kitchen boasted every appliance or gadget to help whip up the full Thanksgiving turkey dinner or just the simple fare that they enjoyed tonight. The meal was just as delightful as the people who were enjoying it. Dora was entertained with stories of Andi's past with her mom and dad and siblings, and Maddie was filled with a wonder of familiar warmth whenever her mother spoke lovingly of her past. It's the rest of the story that was always forbidden in front of Maddie. She didn't need to know the rest yet.

They were all relaxing in the living room now where Maddie was entertaining them with her newest piece on the piano. She was a natural, and it showed in her ability. When Dora said, "Push over," they played together the next several selections duet style, with Dora leading the way and Maddie following easily. It turned into a fun evening ending with instructions and directions for meeting at the hospital in the morning. Things were beginning to get underway.

With the morning meet and greet over, Dora was led to an examining room where she was injected with her first dose of chemo and sent home with instructions of rest and drink plenty of water. Richard was her knight in shining armor. He was her comforter as well as her driver for the next two weeks. That examination room was her 8:30 a.m. four-wall companion for the next two weeks. The next day was a repeat of the first, and so on and so on. After four days of chemo, Dora was feeling no ill effects and no headache or nausea. To everyone's relief, Dora and Richard were able to travel around, sightseeing, catching the matinees downtown, visiting the indoor flea markets, and generally make a mini vacation of their time around Worcester and the greater Boston area. She was still feeling no ill effects after day 11, and Dora's only complaint was she was tired of drinking so much water.

Andi assured her that it was exactly that which had kept her from feeling ill with no mouth sores or too many headaches.

Over the length of these two weeks, they had had many meals at Andi's house as well as a few lunches out, the four of them. It was blood that brought them together, but it was love and respect that developed a bond that could only be called family. So with the chemo injections complete, the transfer date was fast approaching. Both patients were ready and due to be prepped for the transfer in three days. Richard couldn't tell who was more nervous or anxious, Dora, Maddie, or Andi. He felt like the coach with the pep talk and the calming steady voice. So three days before the procedure, both Dora and Maddie were admitted to the hospital for monitored meals, fluid intake, oxygen levels, and blood pressure, along with heart and stress levels. Any number of things could still go wrong, but with the positive attitudes both had, along with the care they were receiving from everyone, all systems were a go.

Once the procedure was underway, the two participants were anxious and willing. Dora and Maddie were lying next to one another on their own gurney, hooked by lines of tubes going every which way. The procedure lasted about three hours, during which time the two patients talked and learned more about each other's past. They were becoming fast buddies. When the steady sound of bellowing air being sucked from one tube to the other stopped, and the stocking-looking cap on the top of Dora's machine collapsed, a new buzzing sound filled the room, which indicated the timing device had stopped and ceased all operations. Procedure complete. No complications and no complaints from either patient for the past three hours. A sense of relief and satisfaction washed over Andi as she realistically reviewed all the facts and stats in both charts of both of her patients. A shower and good meal were next for both of them, and then the testing on Maddie began.

At the end of the day, when once again everyone was gathered at Andi's house for dinner, the relief washed over everyone for a job well done, well received, and really, really appreciated. The discussion worked its way to when Dora and Richard would be leaving and when Andi and Maddie were going to visit them in Arizona.

Dora's medical records would travel with her back to Arizona, where she would need her blood to be checked every month for the next six months. It was just a precaution, nothing to worry about. But with all that chemo flowing through her veins, blood levels needed to be checked to make sure new blood cells were manufactured and distributed to dilute the chemo effects.

Maddie's blood would need to be checked on a daily basis for the first two weeks then a weekly basis to make sure the new cells were adhering and multiplying properly. Weekly testing would need to continue for at least three months before a satisfactory blood count could be registered. It could take up to six or more months before the operation could be deemed a complete success. Just in case, Dora had left behind a few pints of blood in case a transfusion was needed.

Dr. Gayle

It was almost back to normal four months later. Andi was just about to finish her rounds when she heard a page to meet a VIP in her office. She was confused and curious enough to get there immediately to see to this mystery. It was with great pleasure that Dr. Gayle Hampshire was standing in the doorway, waiting for Andrea to arrive. Their meeting was an eruption of hugs and tears and love. All this grew out of the respect Andi had for Dr. Hampshire since they met thirteen years ago and subsequently all her tutoring and mentoring and guidance since. Andi and Gayle fell into an easy conversation of getting caught up, and then Gayle congratulated Andi on her work with the stem cell procedure with her daughter. Gayle admitted that she looked in on Maddie's file and was up-to-date with her progress.

"Ya know, Andi, you were one of my most integrating cases way back when. When you weren't sleeping at night, neither was I. I couldn't image myself going through what you were going through. Therefore, how was I going to be able to help you?"

"You were so openly blunt and—" Andi started.

Gayle stopped her with "Please let me finish. I'm almost ashamed of myself for taking so long to initiate this conversation. I've not let the open police files on your ordeal thirteen years ago rest. I am so glad that you found Dora to help you with Maddie's plight, but remember there was another blood type that came back with similar family trait numbers?"

This time, Gayle did sit back and openly watched Andi's face register shocked confusion. Finally, Gayle said, "You do know that there are still three open cases from that night of the fire?"

Andi just stared at her, waiting for her to continue speaking, too stunned to formulate any thoughts.

Gayle continued, "One, who set the fire. Two, who raped you. Three, who was the unidentified dead body by the garage? I think all three are connected. That is why not one of them has been solved or even come close to being solved." Gayle took a long breath. "You must think I'm nuts standing here with these thoughts. Did you know I was only thirty-four years old when you became my patient? That's about the age you are now...right?"

This time, Andi did speak forcefully and wouldn't take no for an answer. "Come on, Gayle, we're going home. We're going to have a stiff drink, some food, and a lot of talk. I need you to get all of this off your mind. No, off your shoulders. I think you have been carrying this far too long. Let's go."

Gayle grabbed her bag, jacket, and Andi's arm. Lights off and away they went. Andi insisted to drive the nine miles to her home. Gayle did not put up a fuss, just got in the front seat of Andi's car. And within minutes, they were pulling into the driveway of 18 Robin's Nest Drive. Again, Andi was struck with the pleasure and pride she had in her home. Even Gayle complimented Andi on her home.

Within minutes, the two women were seated in the kitchen, now dusk outside, with Southern Comfort Whiskey sours, large ones, and talking about old times with a pork tenderloin, carrots, and potatoes in the oven due to be ready in about an hour.

Finally, they moved to the TV room, and Andi said, "Okay, spill your guts. From the beginning. I need to know what you know and what you've been thinking about all these years. No holds barred. I can take it now."

Gayle was finally ready to breach this subject and get Andi involved with possibly finding another family member. "Okay," she started. "We are both doctors, and we both have a badge. We need to start with the unidentified male lost to the fire that night. Did you know his DNA numbers were close to Dora's but even higher? Did you know the DNA testing done on your vaginal fluids immediately after you were raped and other scrapings from your skin, like behind your ears where he may have lapped or between your toes where he sucked, also were the same as the body by the garage? I can't believe the police didn't do more with this information and dig a little more to identify this person. But then again, how could he have been with you and still set the fire and perish there?"

Gayle looked at her glass. It was empty.

Andi got up from her seat and refreshed both drinks. Her head was spinning, not because of the booze but rather the subject and the fact she hadn't thought about that night for so long. Now it was back in a big way!

"I'm sorry that this is opening painful wounds all over again, but until there are more answers, you can't get on with your life. I've seen you in social situations over the years. I guess I still look at you as my patient. Until you can learn to let your walls down and become more transparent, no one can get close to you. You are still a young and very beautiful woman. Your posture attracts attention, and you dismiss approaches without regard of other people's feelings. If this continues, your reputation will be one of a very cold old lady. As your friend and your doctor, I can't sit back and do nothing and let that happen to you. There, my guts have been spilled. Can you still take it?" Gayle just looked at Andi with hope and apology in her eyes.

"Ya know, I met a very good-looking man when I was in Arizona. I invited his hospitality, one, because it got me a better room in his hotel. And second, because I like coffee with Baileys. Once I drank my coffee, I was very short with him, almost on the brink of rudeness. That I realized once I was back in the safety of my room. Then the next day, I used the closing of the elevator door as my escape from his advances. When I think about it, what I really wanted was for him to push me against the wall and kiss the loving shit out of me. I haven't felt like that in a long time." Andi just looked at Gayle, who was smiling and tapping her fingers on her tall glass. "Is that honest enough for you, Doctor?" Andi needed to get the dig in!

At that, they both moved into the kitchen, retrieved the meal from the oven, sat at the counter bar, and ate and talked the night away.

The next day at work, Andi made a point to seek Gayle out and again make plans to start their own investigation, first into the blood sample and follow that wherever it might lead.

Andi started her quest right here in the hospital lab. Karen Posner, head of the clinical laboratory, who had been such a great help with Maddie's procedure, was anxious to help in any way. However, the lab results and subsequent reports, as old as they are, are now in Boston in the Microfiche SystemDepartment at Mass General. "They are accessible, but you need to have the proper credentials, which you do, and make an appointment to have access."

Gayle was excited at the prospect of going to Boston. "We'll make it a day out. First a little shopping on the way out, lunch, and then the hospital. How long has it been since you've had a day off? This isn't a day off. Let's call it a personal day. We need it. It could be fun."

Andi just looked at her friend and knew she was excited about the adventure. "Okay, I'll make the call and get the appointment. Any restrictions?"

Gayle simply said, "Not on a Monday. Other than that, I'm good to go!"

Back in her own office, Andi made the call to Mass General in Boston and made the appointment to have the films available on Thursday next week. Now she was excited about the venture and the possibility of uncovering clues or facts that had been so far overlooked or not looked at, at all. It was time she admitted to herself that she knew the secrets that the time shell could disclose. The scars had healed over and would not bleed again at any disclosure. But rather, they could heal the open wounds that still needed to be closed. For the first time in many years, she was excited to get to the truth and uncover the nasty facts that took so much from her.

On Thursday morning, Gayle was all business. She picked Andi up in an unmarked car, and they headed for Boston.

"What's with the car?" Andi asked with a quizzical smile on her face.

"We are on a mission, and we are going to bring back facts that Grafton didn't know existed. Therefore, why not get paid for it, along with free gas and tolls, and be on the clock at the same time? By the way, you need to sign out when we get back, because you are on the clock as well." Gayle checked the rearview, glanced over at Andi, smiled a wicked smile, and relaxed behind the wheel.

One hour later, they were parked at Mass General and checking in at the security office and talking with Officer Mark Sheridan, who timed them in and escorted them to the Microfiche Systems Department. Within minutes, Gayle and Andi were into films and facts that they didn't know existed. Andi's eye popped at the blood sample that keyed almost exactly the same as Maddie's. Her heart stopped when she read the scanty facts as printed on the card:

> DOA: burned beyond recognition, male, autopsy bone examination age 18–28, removed from fire crime scene at 17 Speer Street, Grafton, MA, on April 12, 1964.

That was all! A life gone, and that was all! To her knowledge, no one had ever inquired about a missing person. He was never identified or missed! The blood had to have more to say. She'd dig into this a little more. It had family traits. It could definitely tell a story. Why was this buried here? Why didn't she know about this before? It was never too late to find the truth!

Gayle was looking at newspaper articles about the fire, the people involved with fighting the fire, the people who had lost their lives in the fire, the investigation into the cause of the fire, and the length of time it remained an open case in Grafton and subsequently became a cold case with no additional leads to be followed up on.

After two hours of scanning hundreds of files, not one word was started about Andi, her ordeal in the orchard, the crime committed against her body, or the fact that she was removed from the house before the fire was started. Andrea Chambers was the only survivor of that horror show listed, and the story just ended. There were no follow-up stories on the merits of Captain Aspen Chambers or the background of famous Nobel Prize winner father of Mrs. Chambers. The lack of files and facts was eye-opening.

There were no medical records beyond those from Dr. Gayle Hampshire expounding the mental and some physical scars left behind on Andrea's case.

Why were the records so ineffectual? Where were the mountains of papers generated by a four-month hospital stay in Andrea's case?

Gayle found the normal newspaper birth announcement of Maddie on January 21, 1965. No bells, no whistles.

Who wanted this case buried? Why was there so little saved in these files on an open case?

With more questions than they had when they left Grafton, Gayle and Andi settled into a large leather booth at Ken's Steak House on Staler Street on their way home. Each woman, with her own notebook, compared questions that needed answers. Having duel qualifications and authority carried a great deal of weight that neither one of them had ever pushed around nor exercised to the fullest extent, but that was about to change.

Over a succulent lunch of beef tips on egg noodles with brandy sauce, Andi's thoughts went to David in Arizona and how much he'd enjoy this lunch and have pride in serving it in his dining room. Her smile was infectious, and Gayle found herself smiling. She didn't know at what.

"Okay, girlfriend, a penny for your thoughts that I know are not related to our notebooks."

Once again, Andi found herself thinking about David and explained that situation and meeting again to Gayle.

It felt good to feel silly and sixteen years old and never been kissed. That's how those thoughts made her feel. The blush also gave away some of her thoughts!

Back at her office, Andi called Chief Adam Fieldings of Grafton Police and made an appointment for her and Gayle to come by at day's end to discuss their lack of finds in Boston. Chief Fieldings was courteous and willing to meet with them both.

Kelly Mint

That afternoon, when Andi and Gayle entered Chief Fieldings's office, they were surprised to see Sergeant James Stricker and Kelly Mint in attendance. Chief Fieldings explained that these two individuals had many man hours and a great interest in the entire 17 Speer Street tragedy.

Andi vaguely remembered Kelly, and Kelly could see the confusion in Andi's eyes, so she immediately closed the distance between them, took Andi's hands, and said, "I untied the knot that was wound around your throat. I was the first one to see the terror and fright in your eyes, the first one to witness your battered and bruised body from head to toe. I was only twenty-three years old and on the job a total of forty-four days. Never again on my watch did I ever want to experience or see such brutality. Since that day, Jim, Sergeant Stricker, and I have tried to piece together some of the ugly facts."

Sergeant Stricker took up the conversation with "That is one of the reasons you didn't find much in Boston. We held back as much of the files as possible, not wanting them to be considered a cold case. If we had known you were heading to Boston, Fieldings or one of us would have told you to hang back."

Gayle, sitting on the edge of her seat, asked, "So after all this time, do you have any leads, any concrete facts or names of people or places we should be looking into?"

Chief Fieldings scheduled a meeting with Stricker, Mint, and two more detectives for 1:00 p.m. the following day with all files and materials collected over the past fourteen years to be present. Putting some closure to this mystery was long overdue!

That night, Andi had dinner with Lynn, Chuck, Maddie, and Lynn's boys to discuss tomorrow's happenings and try to unwind. *Try* was the operative word! Lynn had been kept abreast of all of Andi's adventures. They just hadn't had a chance to shop or hang out or be friends lately. Andi missed those days.

"I promise when we come up with some answers, we'll have a leisurely lunch, and I'll fill you in on everything."

The next day at one, Andi was staring at a whiteboard with maps, pictures, names, time lines, a few new hospital names, blood card results, newspaper clippings from other states, and character witness statements going back years and crossing state lines.

There was very little in the way of physical evidence from the scene. The only thing they came up with was a gray woolen blanket some ten feet away from where they found Andi. That blanket had been annualized and the DNA from the semen cataloged.

Andi needed to sit down. She had no idea investigations had proceeded into this much information. Why didn't she know? Why wasn't she a part of this? Her education and position in the police department and on the board of human behavioral tendencies should have allotted her a sneak peek at these findings. She was in tears and let herself be a victim again.

Kelly jumped up and hugged Andi, trying to explain that most of what was on the board, she had dug up.

"It took me years to compile some of this information, but once I had...I knew I needed to share it with someone. I was so shaken and upset by your predicament as a professional, being summoned for your care, I needed to swallow hard, tend to you, then go home and fall apart. Thank God for my mom and Jim Stricker, whom I called for help. I knew I couldn't let the attack on you go unpunished." Kelly took a deep breath, got down on her knees in front of Andi, and said, "I was raped when I was fourteen years old, living in Merriment, New Hampshire. That's when my folks moved here. We are going to solve your case, and we are both going to feel free."

Andi hugged her back!

Déjà Vu

Over the next month, Andi and Gayle collaborated on the blood cards and the hospitals in New York. Their credentials opened a lot of doors and loosened a lot of lips. Knowing New York was going to be their next stop, they both put in for a one-week work-related furlough to expand their search and not let a door close again on this investigation.

After gathering as much information they could on the location at which they found R. Sabers's blood card, they were off and ready to learn. In the meantime, it was a great time for Maddie to stay with Auntie Lynn again and play with the boys.

Hazel, a sixty-six year old semi-retired nurse from Samaritan Hospital, laughed and recalled the two boys. They were selling their blood, trying to scrape enough money together to buy gas to get home to Towson, Maryland, for Thanksgiving.

"That was the first time they came in. But after that, I needed to educate them on the time line for withdrawing their blood to stay healthy. I think that's when they started looking at other hospitals for their scheme. Ya know what…one year when they got back to school, they actually came in and donated their blood for a drive that was posted for post-holiday shortages. They made sure I knew about it!" That was a long time ago.

Gayle asked, "Do you keep records of the donors' names, address, blood type? Do you know where these two went to school?"

"Sure, I can put you in touch with the gal who runs that department for the Red Cross, and I know they can help with that."

Andi and Gayle went down two floors and found Ms. Harper, who already knew they were coming.

"Sign here," she said. And then more information than they knew existed from many years back were put in front of them. The name Rockwell, for some reason, rang a bell in Andi's brain, or it being an unusual name, she just thought on it a minute and shook her head. His blood type…he was the one. With shaking hands, Andi withdrew the card from her valise and sure enough, R. Saber. Same name and address, blood drive of January 1964, student at RPI, home residence, Towson, Maryland.

Andi dug a little deeper in her valise and found the first file on Dora. Tucked in the folder was a copy of the blood card on Rockwell Saber, Troy, New York, and the long-lost letter from the Red Cross with his home information regarding the drive in January 1964.

While tugging on Gayle's arm, trying to get her attention, Andi looked up and saw Hazel trying to get her attention. All eyes were on Hazel now. She said, "Way back when these guys were selling their blood—yes, two of them—one of them went missing, I remembered and found this poster that they put up all around the school. The real good-looking one almost went to pieces when the other one, you know, Mr. Sabers, disappeared. I don't think he was ever found. That was a long time ago, May 1964, but I remember it like yesterday. The big blood drives are always around or right after the holidays."

"Hazel, what was the other man's name, the good-looking one? Did he donate blood or sell his blood as well?"

"I know he did. *Oh*, he was a ladies' man. Let me think…I'll remember."

Gayle and Andi had their heads together and felt as though they had really come up with something. It felt right. They needed to dig more into Mr. Sabers, and they needed to know his friend's identity. Without a name, the blood cards were just dots and numbers, and after a few hours of studying this information, everything started to look the same. Deciding to break for lunch, Andi and Gayle were leaving the hospital, walking past Hazel's desk. She jumped up and yelled, "Kevin! That's his name…Kevin."

Over lunch, Andi decided Towson, Maryland, was going to be her next destination. Gayle agreed. "I'm on board for that. If it weren't you and Maddie, I'd be enjoying this."

Andi felt close to something, something more than she ever had in the past. Andi didn't want to stop looking. She felt on the brink of discovering the next thing that would bring her closer to finding out the entire truth of April 12, 1964. She was sure now that there was more to the devastating fire and more to her injuries and rape.

Other things had taken priority in Andrea's life for the last fourteen years, so thinking about herself or the fire and actually putting people or names and these people's families and feelings into play never really happened. Her career choices were driven by her past and her losses, but this was the first time in a very long time that she could see, could feel her authority driving her to solving these crimes.

After driving for nearly five hours and settling in at a Motel 6 in Towson, Maryland, Andi called back to St. Samaritan Hospital and asked for Ms. Harper. Having left for the day, she left instructions to all hands to be helpful if Andi called back. Andi's questions were of Kevin's last name, blood type, and home address. These items were at the fingertips of Carl, and he was eager to share. Feeling very satisfied, Andi and Gayle ventured out to the neighborhoods, looking for Lost Road. How appropriate. They felt lost and also felt quite tired from their long day. They decided to call it a night and check in with the police in the morning.

After a quick call home to Maddie, Andi talked with Lynn to assure her she was fine, and for once, the search was going in the right direction. Lynn and Chuck were her lifelines and anchors. As strong as she was in many things, it felt like her life was in their hands.

Mickey Levi, police chief of Towson, was happy to meet with Andi and Gayle the next day. His office was streamlined and modern in every way, with old files on computer by date and cross-referenced by name. Finding Rockwell Saber was easy, and along with him was his sidekick, Kevin Schaffer. There were finally pictures to go along with the names. Andi felt a familiar and uneasy draw to both of these men. There were no criminal backgrounds connected to these individuals, but there were watch tags on Schaffer after the disappearance of Sabers. There was a search, by the Troy police, of the apartment shared by Rockwell and Kevin in their due diligence when Rockwell disappeared. In doing so, they found letters addressed to no one and never sent, notes, and scribbling. Kevin admitted writing. He became despondent, withdrawn, and suicidal. Now fourteen years later, he was finally a stable adult with a career in secondary education.

Andi and Gayle got permission, and after signing their life away, they took many of the old files back to their motel and examined them completely. This led them to need to speak with Kevin Schaffer and the parents of Rockwell Sabers. A quick call to Chief Levi had him on board in making the calls.

Upon the return of the files to the police station the next morning, an appointment with Rhonda Sabers had already been made for later that morning, and he was expecting a call back from Alice Schaffer.

"One thing before you meet Rhonda Sabers. Mr., or should I say Captain Sabers, died in 1964. He never knew about his son." Chief Levi scratched his chin, shook his head, and said, "The year 1964 seems to have been a bad year and keeps being a recurring item in all your tragedies and searches."

"How did Captain Sabers die?" asked Gayle while the chief was reaching for the ringing phone on his desk. He held up a "wait a minute" finger to Gayle.

He was all smiles. The chief said that was Mrs. Schaffer, and she had already reached out to Kevin, and he could be at her house by one thirty that afternoon.

"That will give us time to speak with Rhonda Sabers, grab a quick lunch, and resume our questions at the Schaffers. I'm glad Kevin is on board. Everything will be firsthand with him," Chief Levi added.

Gayle answered the chief's unasked question lurking in his eyes by saying, "Nurse Hazel at St. Samaritan said Rockwell's sidekick was the handsome one, a real ladies' man."

"That he is, says most women in our little town. I don't think he ever settled down. Teaches at an all-boys school in…Carney…next town over, Armstrong Academy for Boys. I've been on the job here in town since 1966. Missed the growing up of the boys in question and the goings-on here in 1964. But according to the papers, Captain Sabers's autopsy was done in New Hampshire. Ashes sent back here for burial. The autopsy files are sealed at the Army base in Newport News, Virginia. So cause of death has never been disclosed. Just died on duty, serving his country. The paper said his family would receive all military benefits due him. I believe Mrs. Sabers lives a comfortable life. Let's go visit her."

So the two women from Grafton, Massachusetts, followed Chief Mickey Levi out to his car and were driven to 5 Lost Road to visit Rhonda Sabers.

After driving through a very modern downtown Towson, with its double-lane major route 28 heading north and south through the city with streetlights every two miles at shopping center intersections, banks, churches, three school buildings, and a fire station, turning on to Peaks, then on to Lost Road, it felt as though they had reached the end of the earth.

Lost Road was still a hard-packed dirt road and dead-end after passing four houses. Number 5 was the last one on the road that had a beautiful background of large mature oak, pine, and maple trees. The house wasn't so bad either. Its bungalow shape had a new chimney, windows, and siding. When they pulled in front and stopped, a very attractive woman in her upper years greeted them in the front yard. Once invited in, they walked through a cathedral ceiling living room to a large kitchen with a large kitchen table, where they were made comfortable with coffee and a store-bought strudel. All the fixings for their coffee were on a large lazy Susan in the center of the table.

After all the introductions and simple coffee talk, Andi started with questions about Rockwell, his younger life, college, the blood drives, and then his disappearance. Apologizing for dredging all this up again, Andi assured Mrs. Sabers her answers could hold some very important information for her.

Rhonda said, "First, call me Rhonda. It's been a long time since I've talked about Rockwell. I rather enjoy doing so. Rockwell should have been born a girl. As manly and good-looking as he was…even in his glasses, he was also softhearted and caring in all ways. His respect for me and his protective manner inside this household was paramount. The other kids loved their other big brother."

Andi interrupted with her question of other kids. "So Rockwell had brothers and sisters?"

Rhonda laughed and said, "He was number two of six. Never marry a military man!"

Andi laughed right back and said, "I'm number two of six. My father was a military man."

Rhonda continued, "Russell was first, then Rockwell, and then came Rachel, then the twins, Ruby and Rose, finally Riley, our baby, now almost sixteen. Poor Reginald, their dad, never saw his crew grow up. I lost him fourteen years ago."

Gayle asked if she had any idea how her husband died.

A shake of the head and one word—"no"—was all Rhonda said.

They moved on to Rockwell's relationship with Kevin and the closeness that existed between the two of them.

"From the day the Schaffers moved in next door, the two boys seemed joined at the hip. They became even closer after Kevin's leg surgeries." Rhonda had a faraway look on her face.

Naturally, now they were getting a parental view and opinion of the two young, then teenage, then college-aged men.

Andi said, "Let's back up to what you said about Kevin's treatment and leg operations."

Rhonda was near tears now. "We were so proud of him. Fourteen years old and enduring test after test and then surgery alongside Kevin to transfer his bone cell plasma because he was a match. It worked, and Kevin beat the cancer they found in his leg after he broke it falling out of the tree. Rockwell had his heart healed at the same time. Rockwell blamed himself for Kevin's initial accident that broke his leg and started the whole medical mess. From that day on, the boys healed together and were again inseparable."

The room was silent. Rhonda took a deep breath and continued, "Rockwell's disappearance did a job on Kevin all over again. Poor guy. To this day, we have no idea what happened to Rockwell. But after seven years, we did have him declared dead, had a simple memorial, and were able to put some of our feelings to rest."

Andi had grown quite quiet and still. Her doctor's hat was back on, and she wanted to go back to the police station as soon as they could get there. She thanked Rhonda from the bottom of her heart for opening up and allowing this visit. She needed to check something out ASAP. Chief Levi and Gayle followed Andi's lead and went back to the station to hear Andi out.

Behind closed doors, Andi asked the chief to order up the medical records of both Rockwell and Kevin from where Kevin was operated on. Did Rhonda say?

This could be key. These records held answers.

Chief Levi picked up the phone and called back to Rhonda Sabers's house. "Hello, Rhonda, Chief Levi here. One quick question. What hospital was Rockwell and Kevin in together? Okay, thanks.

"Baltimore General Medical." He picked up the phone again and dialed four. "Donna, call Baltimore General Medical. Get to the Surgical Department and order blood types on both Rockwell Sabers and Kevin Schaffer. Stem cell surgery involving both in 1956. Have that department call back here with the results."

"Okay, Andi, what's up? You are as white as a ghost, and I think you blood pressure is sky-high right now." Gayle walked over to Andi and proceeded to take her pulse.

190

"I read something, somewhere…I can't remember. But I know that when you transfer blood from one to another…like Rockwell to Kevin, Kevin's blood type changes to Rockwell's type. So now when we get the results from Baltimore General, I bet we are going to see both guys with the same blood type, where Kevin's was different at birth. I know that is an answer to one of the major questions we haven't even been able to formulate yet. We are so close. I am so close, but to what? I know now how they have the same blood type, but how is the family variant showing up here? What are we missing?"

These thoughts and questions came rambling out of Andi's brain and mouth as she paced around the room, looking from Gayle to Chief Levi. Neither one of them had the answers she so desperately needed.

The call came from the hospital, and sure enough, Rockwell's and Kevin's 1956 blood types were the same.

Gayle suggested lunch before they went to the Schaffers'. They just had just enough time before one thirty.

A quick lunch at Harry's Pizza and a tall iced tea was just what the doctor ordered. With that, they reviewed the facts as they had them so far. Gayle started with the dual blood types and how ingenious it was for Andi to come up with that. But Andi needed to voice the parallels she had picked up on so far. "Maybe there is nothing to it, but look at this." She starting listing.

MA	MD
military dad	military dad
dead in '64	dead in '64
six kids	six kids
alphabet name	alphabet name

cancer	cancer
same blood	same blood
ere facts…	

"Not ere, interesting. Let's get Levi and go," Gayle urged Andi along.

They pulled up in front of 4 Lost Road, behind a shiny black 1977 Pontiac Firebird.

"Nice wheels," said Gayle. She was much more of a car freak than Andi. They walked toward the front of the house. Voices coming from the back of the house stopped their approach. Andi froze in place. With her hands, she indicated *quiet*…and she continued to listen. Gayle and Levi exchanged questioning glances and waited for Andi to release the stop she had intended. Words were barely discernible, but the tone of voice and the cough and the sharpness of tone when he was agitated was…so familiar. Again, ere with a déjà vu feeling. Andi had the feeling of flight, "get out of here," "let's not do this now," scared!

All of this started to show on her face, and her posture became loose, then she fell to the ground. She was out cold with fright. Levi picked her up and gently placed her in the back seat of the car. Gayle climbed in after her, took her vitals, and softly spoke to her in soothing tones. Meanwhile, Levi had the car heading back to headquarters. Gayle said, "There, not the hospital."

Levi radioed ahead so when they arrived, a gurney was waiting equipped with oxygen. Within minutes, Andi was able to sit up but not explain what had come over her. She apologized, but even in review, she was unable to explain what had brought on such a strong feeling. She fought for a word to explain how she felt.

Gayle was stumped at Andi's reaction to whatever it was!

The only time she had seen anyone—the anyone being Andi—faint like that was when Andi avoided being touched in the hospital or the memory of those bad touches. If they came too close to the surface, she would faint. This was her saving grace, her choice of avoidance! What had brought that on today? On the street, in a chase, facing bank robbers, speaking soothing words to a mother after a horrific car crash where she was losing her son...but never this reaction. So why now?

All of a sudden, Andi requested Chief Levi to invite the Schaffers here to the station. "We've scheduled with them for today. Kevin made the effort to come to town. Please call and ask them to come here. If need be, use me as an excuse."

Levi was happy to do so, except for Andi's health. "Are you sure you're okay?"

"I'll be just fine. Now that I know I'm jumpy or agitated by something here, I'll be on the lookout for clues at what may set me off. Let's call it an education in déjà vu."

"You get those feelings too?" Levi asked with a change to his voice. "I was told that was good police work, but, girl, you've got to stop fainting whenever they overcome you."

For the first time in many minutes, that caused a laugh, and it enabled Levi to make the call to the Schaffers and move the meeting there.

Thirty minutes later, Mr. and Mrs. Schaffer, Kevin, Chief Levi, Gayle, and Andi were sitting around a conference table, trying to make believe this was not official police business. Coffee was offered, ice water was on the table, each had a steno pad and pen, and nervousness set in on all occupants.

Andi tried to lighten the room with her introduction. "I'm afraid this is getting off on the wrong foot. No need for nerves. I'm Andrea Chambers. This is Gayle Hampshire, and we are doctors from Massachusetts with questions stemming from the fact that you, Kevin, since your cancer surgery and stem cell exchange with Rockwell Sabers, have the same blood type as my daughter back in Massachusetts. We are doctors and find that fact very confusing and just needed to meet you and maybe discuss your college days."

That just came out. Andi had no idea where she was going to go from there, but she continued, "We met Nurse Hazel at St. Samaritan Hospital. You and Rockwell made quite an impression on her. She still remembers the pair of you to this day."

Kevin just stared at her. Now it was his turn to feel queasy and uncomfortable.

Mr. Schaffer asked, looking between Andrea and Gayle, "What are you trying to discover with your inquisition of Kevin and Mrs. Sabers? The past had bad vibes and holds terrible memories. We all would rather it be left in the past."

"Then again, I'll thank you for seeing us today, but I need to ask Kevin if he or Rockwell ever donated their stem cell plasma to anyone else while in college...you know, for a fee or a fiend in need?" That said, she looked straight at Kevin and waited for an answer.

Andi took a deep breath and thought, *Where did that come from?* She was feeling more confident now. She returned her attention to Kevin. "Well?"

"I remember the only time Rockwell..." He repeated, "Only time Rockwell donated stem cell, it hurt like hell. He said only for me would he go through such hell. So, *no*, neither of us ever donated stem cell in college or any other time…other than for me."

Chief Levi then asked, "Do you have any idea at all what happened to Rockwell? Do you know of anyone who would have wanted to do him harm? Was he involved in anything that would have caused his disappearance or his death? Do you know if drugs were involved with him or his acquaintances?"

Now the room was very uncomfortable and very silent.

This time, it was Mrs. Schaffer who spoke up. "This is the past my husband was talking about. We've been over this ground before, with no to all of your questions. Nothing has changed in that regard over the past fourteen years. It has taken a good many of those years for all of us to begin to live normal healthy lives again, so please go back to Massachusetts and leave us alone."

Gayle had been patient and still long enough. She made eye contact with every person in the room, put her hands palm down on the table, and proceeded to speak. "There is something that happened that Rockwell and Kevin were both privy too. I believe that is a fact. I believe that Rockwell died with his secrets, but I also believe that Kevin still doesn't sleep good at night remembering his or Rockwell's secrets. I am a clinical criminal physiologist, and I am very good at my job. So, yes, we will go back to Massachusetts, but you've given us a lot to bring back to study on.

"Furthermore, Kevin, if you'd like to start sleeping better at night, we can be reached until noon tomorrow, at which time we leave this city. But rest assured, we will talk again! Dr. Chambers, with me, please." Gayle ushered Andi from her seat, opened the door, and they both left.

"What? What is it, Gayle?" Andi asked, confused.

"Come on. We need another private room."

Gayle took Andi by the hand, and they continued down the hall, took a left, and entered an empty conference room. Gayle closed the door and told Andi to take a seat and get comfortable.

She turned around, faced Andi, and asked, "You tell me. What is it about Kevin that has your personal panties all tied up? That wasn't a professional interrogation in there. That was personal!"

After a long pause, Andi admitted that something about Kevin did turn her inners to a queasy mess. "His voice, a sound he makes, his self-assured attitude, the way he looks at me."

Gayle admitted she also saw the way he looked at Andi, like he was trying to place her somewhere, like he'd seen her before somewhere.

"Do you think you've ever seen him before?" Gayle asked Andi. "It almost sounds like maybe you have. He looks at you the same way." Now Gayle dragged a chair closer to Andi and watched her face as she spoke.

"We just asked those people in there to relive something that happened fourteen years ago, and you just asked me to do the same. Some old memories hurt...just like they said."

Gayle continued with her doctor voice, reached out, and took Andi's hands in hers. "Are you thinking about fourteen years ago? Go ahead and close your eyes. Are you in the orchard, listening? Don't feel, just listen. Did you hear a voice today that you've heard before?" Gayle paused. "Place that voice close to your ear. You can't see. All your bodily senses need to lead you to your assailant." Gayle was talking very slowly now, pausing to let her words sink in. "His cheek is on your belly." Andi squeezed Gayle's hands. "Do you feel smooth hair...curly hair? Is his voice low toned or high toned? When he mounts you..." Andi dropped Gayle's hands and wrung her fingers together. "Does he have a long body or short body? Listen again. Does he talk? Street talk or educated? Any names?"

"Wait...wants to take a picture...put it in the bag...your mother...show Rockwell for revenge." Andi jumped to her feet and faced Gayle. "Rockwell...that's the name! I knew as different as it is, I've heard it before."

"Sit down. That's good. Close your eyes again. Relax and go back into the orchard. You said, 'Wants to take a picture.' Who wants to take a picture?" Gayle was trying to lead Andi back into long suppressed memories and maybe get to the bottom of some of the old hurtful secrets.

Andi couldn't sit still now. She went farther down the long conference table and sat facing a pencil and pad of paper. She began to write. "Kevin wanted to take a picture to show Rockwell. They needed revenge against his father. They were doing it the same way his father did against his mother...add picture in the bag? I'm pretty sure those are the words he used." By now, Andi had her head in her hands.

Gayle walked to the end of the table where Andi was sitting and asked, "Andi, you said Kevin. Do you think that is Kevin talking?" The two women just stared at each other, "May I read what you've written?"

Andi handed Gayle the pad of paper and listened as Gayle read it out loud. They were just words running together. They didn't make any sense.

Gayle reminded Andi that she lost consciousness often during her attack, that maybe she didn't hear all the words, or Kevin was just thinking out loud and didn't say all the words.

"May I read it again with punctuation and give it meaning?" Gayle questioned Andi.

"Go for it. What can it hurt?"

"I wish I could take a picture to show Rockwell that I have taken revenge on his father, not to hurt his mother, and we'll add the picture to the bag." Gayle looked at Andi with a question across her brow.

"I remember he said, 'The pictures in the bag are a secret.' So many questions...so few answers. I'd love to see the bag of pictures." Andi looked at Gayle and said, "The more I think I remember, I do think it was Kevin. Heaven help me if I'm wrong, but for the first time in fourteen years, I think we have a suspect. I really didn't know what we were going to find coming down here to Maryland, but my rapist, Maddie's sperm donor...does Maddie really have grandparents? Like I said, *sooo* many questions."

Gayle walked over and started massaging Andi's shoulders. "You know what you have to do next, what any victim is asked to do... what any cop always does. You need to do both! I can help with the cop part. I'll look over your shoulder as you write the victim portion and develop my questions from those comments and observations." Gayle stepped away from Andi then sat down beside her. "Looks like we are going to be in Maryland a little longer."

It was nearing dinnertime, and both women needed a telephone. First, they left a message for Chief Levi with his secretary then proceeded to the squad room and available telephones. Andi needed to call or talk with her daughter, but contact with Lynn would be second best, and Gayle needed to contact the hospital and make sure their department was still functioning well without them. With that accomplished, dinner was next.

They drove their car out of visitor parking to a golden neon blinking light advertising an all-you-can-eat Chinese food buffet. Once seated with their choice of alcoholic beverage, they both let their thoughts wander. Silently, fourteen years ago came back to both of them, each on the same subject but with different pictures running through their heads.

Andi was meeting Dr. Gayle Hampshire for the first time and could picture her telling her that her parents and all the kids died in a house fire, her house. In those moments, her body, the one that hurt all over, didn't matter anymore. Now, fourteen years later, she had learned how to live without her family, and it was time to get to the truth of the other ordeal. She had never thought about her rapist having a family. A mom and dad and, by now, possibly a wife and children of his own. Young boys grow up, straighten out, change. Had Kevin? She knew he wasn't married with children, and she had met his mom and dad. Did that change the fact of what he had done to her? She reached for her drink that was already gone and decided, no…certain acts definitely had consequences.

Gayle was just ordering their second round of drinks after thinking about the young girl who just found out she was pregnant after being violently raped by an unknown attacker. That poor girl had just lost her entire family in a house fire. Her support system was gone just when she needed them the most. Was Kevin her attacker? Was Rockwell involved with this in any way?

Kevin and Rockwell were best friends. What did Rockwell's dad have to do with Kevin, thinking about him during his act of violence? Where was Rockwell?

With the second round of drinks in hand, the women shared their thoughts and knew they had their work cut out for them.

Tomorrow, they'd start digging in Andi's memories and talk with Kevin again. Dinner was tasty and ample. They had variations of many chicken, beef, and pork dishes. The rice and noodles were also very plentiful. Chinese vegetables were always a treat at these buffets.

Andi said, "If you leave hungry, it's your own fault."

Once back in their motel, Andi called home again, this time needing to talk with Maddie. A bit of motherly love needed reinforcing. She needed to hear her daughter's voice and hear about her day. That was always enough to take the edge off a stressful day. Today was one of those days. She knew sleep would be a dreadful event tonight because she needed to dredge up, remember, and write up a victim's account of fourteen years ago. The more she thought about it, the more she truly believed she was on the right track.

The next day, back at the police station, Chief Levi was brought up-to-date on Andi's thinking. He agreed that it was time for her to write up the victim's statement, as painful as it was going to be, and he and Gayle would visit with Kevin again. Andi was led to a conference room again. It looked the same as the one she was in yesterday, complete with a pad of paper and a pencil. But this time, she had a policewoman standing at the door.

"I am Officer Hayden. Frances, if you like. Just let me know if you need anything. We could send out for coffee and donuts, or could I get you some water?" the officer asked.

"No, not now. Thanks for asking. I'm Andrea. Just call me Andi, but I think I need to get to work." With that, Andi sat, picked up the pencil, and wrote. She wrote and continued writing and wrote some more. The night came alive in her mind. After seven or eight pages into her memories, coffee did arrive, along with a warm damp cloth and an order to take a break, drink, and wipe her brow.

She did as she was told. A long swig of coffee, followed by a cleansing wipe across her face with the soothing warm cloth, relaxed her mind and brought her back to the present.

"Thank you kindly, Frances Hayden. I needed that! Are Chief Levi and Dr. Hampshire back yet?"

"They are not. Is there anything else I can do for you?"

"Indeed. I need to make a couple of calls back to my chief in Massachusetts. Show me the way. It will feel good to stretch my legs after sitting there all this time. How long was I sitting there writing?" Andi asked.

Opening the door and walking down the hall, Officer Hayden informed Andi that she had been writing for nearly two hours. "I could tell some of what you were writing was pretty intense, so I figured coffee would help."

"Your figuring was right on. Thanks again," Andi said as they entered the squad room. She was led to an empty desk and a telephone.

Andi's first call was to her secretary at the medical center. All was calm, with no fires to put out. Her second call was to Chief Adam Fieldings, Grafton Police Department.

"Chief, this is Andrea Chambers, I'm in Towson, Maryland, with Dr. Gayle Hampshire, and we've come across a number of items relevant to my abduction and maybe even hints to the house fire. What I need, please, is a copy of the autopsy report on the eighth victim in the fire."

Just then, Andi looked up and saw Gayle and Chief Levi enter the room. Gayle headed over to Andi immediately and eased-dropped at the end of her conversation.

"Yes, sir, that report, as it should also have his blood type listed. Yes, sir, that number is…and thank you again. Bye.

"I contacted Chief Fieldings at home and requested the autopsy report on body number eight from the fire." Andi looked at Gayle and continued, "I learned a lot from my own writing this morning. I'm really anxious to share it with you. So how did you two make out?" Andi made eye contact with Gayle and Chief Levi.

Chief Levi took the lead. "Without you in the room, Kevin was an entirely different person. He was professional, polite, and seemed sincerely interested in trying to help. He was relaxed and answered our questions without hesitance. I do understand that after fourteen years, he doesn't remember some things. At least I'd like to believe him when he says that. But as a cop, I think he is using the fourteen-year statement to his benefit and using that statement to hide behind. That young man remembers and knows more than he is saying. I also believe that he used last night to practice his deceit of today."

Gayle concurred with Chief Levi about Kevin's demeanor around them this morning. "He definitely knows more than he is saying. We'll get it out of him. One way or the other, with the right questions and the right probing, he'll fold. You know why? Because his parents are honorable people, and I think they raised him right. Somewhere, he took a wrong turn. Deep down, he wants to makes things right!" Gayle said this with feelings and determination.

Now Andi was excited to share with them all that she had written this morning and what she was looking for in the autopsy of number 8. All of her thinking had also given rise to questions that needed answers. Maybe Maryland had those answers. They could possibly be found on the dead-end street. She knew for a fact that they, or at least she, would be going back there to talk with Mrs. Sabers and the Schaffers once again.

Gayle and Andi once again returned to the conference room that had become their office away from home. Andi read the notes from the morning spent with the Schaffers and felt as though she was being lead down a path of "I'd love to help you, but I don't recall" bullshit!

While Andi was reading Gayle's notes, Gayle was reading Andi's notes that were written that morning.

"I'm impressed," Gayle said.

"It ended up taking a lot out of me, but once the juices of memory were unlocked, they flowed easily on to the paper. There is so much we need to look into. But first for the facts…"

My assailant was tall…when he laid on top of me…he was long. He felt lean and a little muscular.

He had his longish hair in a ponytail. I remember trying to pull his hair before he tied by hands behind my back.

His hair felt smooth, not curly.

He had a masculine, authoritative, professional voice…educated, not vulgar.

At the time, no facial hair. No mustache or beard.

He wore a chain around his neck.

His hands felt big.

He smelled of beer but not cigarettes.

He referred to his car by name...a girl's name, but I don't remember it.

What revenge?

What pictures?

Where are the picture now?

Double-check whose blood changed in the stem cell exchange. Did Kevin's change to Rockwell's? Or the other way around?

How is Kevin's blood type like Maddie's?

Test the Schaffers' blood.

Test the Sabers' blood.

Examine autopsy of number 8 from fire.

Blood type...Rockwell?

Captain Sabers...dead fourteen years...1964.

Rockwell missing...dead fourteen years, 1964.

Ask to see Sabers separation papers. Who signed, how much $

See if any military personnel names are the same as on Chambers.

Dig deeper into alpha names of kids, Sabers, Chambers.

Try to get personal records, leave time, duty stations on both captains.

Can Kevin be extradited back to Massachusetts?

Gayle was still reading Andi's notes when Chief Levi knocked on the door. "Can we be of help to you two?" he asked, walking into the room.

"I think maybe you can," Andi answered quickly. Gayle handed Levi Andi's notes. "I now think with the proper interrogation, here at the police station, after he has been read his Miranda rights, we've got Kevin nailed! Abduction and statutory rape of a minor carries what for a sentence?" Andi inquired.

Chief Levi ran his figures through his hair. "By golly, young lady, I think you might have something here!"

"I think our being here has upset his equilibrium. He has skated along for these fourteen years, not having to pay the piper for his nasty deeds, and now that is all he can think about. I'll bet he is close to breaking. We ask the right questions and his tongue will let loose," Gayle added.

"Okay." Chief Levi was on board. "Who gets first crack at him?"

Gayle spoke up very fast. "It's you and me, Chief. Andrea's too close to this case and personally involved. It wouldn't be good for her to question this man."

"I agree. Go have lunch, review Andi's notes, and turn them into questions. We'll use them to unsettle him. If he's on the defensive, he'll slip up. They always do. We can put our heads together at two p.m. I'll have Kevin Schaffer brought in for questioning around four p.m. by two uniformed officers. We'll be ready for him. We'll do this together."

At 2:00 p.m., Gayle and the chief were in a huddle, and the fax from Massachusetts came in with what Andi had requested on number 8. She was in a hurry to study its contents and hopefully learn and be led down a path of more pertinent questions. She started reading:

> With the condition of the remains found on the grounds of 17 Speer Street, Grafton, Massachusetts, approximately twelve feet behind a two-car garage and three feet in front of a fence that was also scorched from the fire, this is a site of a horrendous house fire, they could tell very little with certainty. What they did know was his blood type and DNA was a match to the Chambers. He was six foot one tall in his early twenties. His last meal was primarily beer, which had been boiled away from the fire, but it left a distinct lining in this stomach. There were fingerprints lifted at the scene, one from the roof of a burnt car and prints from the gate behind the garage. There were only two fingers on the deceased that could be printed. But neither one of those were a match from the scene.

Andi was thinking and making notes as she was reading. *Need to fingerprint Kevin.*

Deep in thought with her mind on her own project, she nearly missed the two uniformed officers escorting Kevin to an interrogation room somewhere down the hall. Trying to get back to the project at hand was impossible now. She asked to be shown to a viewing room to watch and listen to Kevin's interrogation. She also asked for a chair. She knew how weak-kneed she could become. Gayle was right. This was very personal for her.

Before Chief Levi and Gayle entered the room where they held Kevin, Andi had the opportunity to watch him, really look at him. Nurse Hazel was right. He was pretty. He had great hair, perfect lips, and high cheekbones that made his eyes smile and gave him an easy, comfortable demeanor. Right now, he shouldn't look that comfortable. His looks and perfectly practiced posture made him look like a poster boy for Valentine's Day.

Give him a box of candy and flowers and "It's Maddie on her tiptoes handing me flowers with her gigantic smile and…*oh* my god. Oh my…oh my!"

Andi couldn't breathe. She felt the tears running down her face. She tried to take deep breaths, calm herself, and look at him again. *Breathe…breathe.*

The door opened, and Gayle could see the anguish on Andi's face.

"Look at him," Andi whispered. "Look at that straight spine, the color of his hair, those eyes that speak above cheekbones that were chiseled by artists. It's Maddie. Oh my god…oh my…"

Gayle wrapped her arms around Andi and let her cry. She encouraged her to cry. This time, it was necessary and cleansing. Gayle had already seen the likenesses and came to the same conclusion. They had their rapist! Now how much he knew about the fire or about Rockwell were their next hurdles to conquer.

Gayle squatted down to be eye level with Andi. "Listen," she said. "We've just fingerprinted Kevin before putting him in that room. Next, Chief Levi and I are going to question him. We've put together quite a few good questions using your list as leads. His answers and comments should be interesting and put us in a position to hold him on suspension or charge him immediately. We also believe that he was complacent in the plans Rockwell had to avenge something for his father. This would make him an accessory to the crime of arson and murder. Are you all right in here?"

Andi just looked at Gayle through watery eyes, grabbed her hands, and squeezed.

"Officer Hayden will be keeping you company. That's the young woman you met this morning, okay?"

With that, the door opened, and Gayle got to her feet. Officer Frances Hayden walked in and greeted Andi like they were going out for lunch. In the next moment, the chief walked in with another chair for Officer Hayden and planted a tissue box in Andi's lap.

"Good eavesdropping," he said. Then he and Gayle left the room.

They looked at the window in front of them. Andi and Officer Hayden saw Gayle and the chief enter the room where Kevin sat.

"Good afternoon, Mr. Schaffer. For the record, let me inform you that this interview is being recorded. Please verbally respond that you were informed and understand."

Kevin looked at Chief Levi and at Gayle for the first time, like he was in trouble. He merely said, "I understand this is being recorded."

"Great!" Gayle jumped right in. "I don't understand the fascination with you guys naming your cars. You drive a black beauty right now. Is that her name, Black Beauty? Or did you use the same one you had before?"

Kevin looked totally confused and amused at her question. He leaned forward a bit and smiled. He rubbed his face with both hands and said, "That's a great name, but I guess I grew up. I don't name my cars anymore. Why did you have me brought here? I need to get back. I have a class to tend to in the morning."

Officer Hayden kept an eye on Andi at all times, as were her instructions at being put in the room with Andi. Gayle didn't know the direction the interrogation was going to take and didn't want Andi to faint alone.

"Okay, to get right to the point," Gayle continued. "Do you still have the pictures Rockwell let you see? Did he give you the story behind them? Are they someplace you can put your hands on them easily?"

Chief Levi jumped in with "Ya know, Rockwell has been gone for a really long time now. Are you still keeping his secrets? Who would they hurt? Does it still matter? Is it worth losing sleep over all these years later?"

Like Gayle, Chief Levi just threw out question after question, just pacing around the room, always looking straight at Kevin, keeping eye contact and waiting for a word or subject to change his facial expression.

"Did you ever share with your parents…no…your mom any of Rockwell's secrets or your escapades with Rockwell or girls when you were in college? Did you ever bring a girl home to meet your mom and dad? Or…do you like boys better? How are they at that school you go to every day?"

At that, Kevin was out of his seat, but before he could charge at the chief, Levi pushed the table toward Kevin hard enough to push Kevin back. He lost his balance and landed back in his chair, up against the wall, pinned by the table at his waist. The temperature in the room went from a little uncomfortable to downright hot!

Andi jumped a mile at the pace in the other room. She took a deep breath and resumed her diligent watch.

"Let's try again." Chief Levi, on the pace again, looked at Kevin straight in the eyes. "Are Rockwell's secrets still in the bag of pictures you so carefully cared for, or did you let them out?"

"Rockwell died because of those pictures and that damn woman." Kevin let out on an angry breath.

"So you knew he was dead. You went through all the motions of a distraught roommate, best friend, buddy, but you kept that secret from everyone. All these years, lying to everyone. You put together the time line, the place, the pictures, the girl, the town, his secret, his anger, the fire. You knew, you yellow-bellied chicken!"

Chief Levi didn't let up. He just kept talking and pacing from one end of the room to the other. All eyes were on him. Kevin's posture was suffering from the barrage of words, as was his stamina to keep his mouth shut.

"I won't talk about Rockwell anymore. What good would it do? He's gone." Everyone was taking a deep breath.

Gayle needed to fill the silence that was starting to happen around them, so she said, "Okay, let's talk about you. The chief posed a question to you that is still unanswered. Do you favor girls or boys?"

Andi whispered, "Oh boy!" and watched intently.

Immediately, they could see his fear starting to rise, but he merely banged the table and said, "Girls."

"Now we're getting somewhere. A straight answer. Do you still have the bag of pictures?"

"No."

"Where are they? What did you do with them?"

"They meant nothing to me. I buried them."

"Where?"

Gayle continued, "They must have meant something to you. You felt Rockwell's anger and helped him light the fire and burn their house to the ground."

Gayle barely finished her sentence, and Kevin rushed in with "I wasn't even there. He lit the fire. I saw flames in the sky. I rushed out of the orchard, and he didn't meet me like he said he would."

Andi sat, stoic, just looking at the window, seeing Kevin fidget in his seat. His eyes were glassy. He was seeing something no one else could see.

Arrest

"Mr. Schaffer, at this point in our conversation, I need to inform you of your rights. You have the right to remain silent and to have an attorney present. If you give up these rights, anything you say can and will be held against you. Do you understand these rights as I have read them to you?"

"Yes, yeah, yeah. Don't you get it? I was so dunk, so sick, so scared, so alone for weeks. I was waiting for him to come home. I read in the paper about all the bodies at the house, but they never did say they found him. I waited for weeks. It was no use. I had to go home. Ya know what?"

"What?" Gayle and Levi said in unison.

"I'm glad I got the girl out. Ya know what else? I didn't need to go to Grafton to see the prettiest girl in the world. She's been living next to me for years. Rachel looks just like the Grafton girl."

"How did you see the pretty girl in Grafton? You covered her head," Gayle asked him directly.

"In her yard that afternoon, when we were comparing the pictures to her house and yard and the surroundings. She was there."

Now Kevin just put his head down on the table and drummed his fingers to a tune in his head. He yawned, and memories started coming out of his mouth.

By now, Andi was standing at the window, feeling that if she were closer, she wouldn't miss anything. Officer Hayden was right beside her.

"I was really nervous standing in her room when the grandfather clock dinged. Then my heart was beating so fast and loud. I figured everyone in the house would hear me. I bent to pick her up, and she screamed. Then I prayed I didn't hit her too hard. I did what I could to shut her up, covered her head, and carried her out. She was a tough little cookie. I really wanted Rachel, but Rockwell would have killed me. He was like a brother to me. His mother is really pretty, but his father was such an ass."

"Mr. Schaffer, at this point, we are placing you under arrest for the act of kidnapping and rape, sexual assault, and attempted murder. Please stand." Chief Levi was even toned but forceful.

"You can't. I have to work tomorrow," Kevin murmured as he was being handcuffed by Gayle.

Chief Levi, again, told Kevin he shouldn't say any more until he had an attorney present, but he wouldn't stop talking.

"No one really knows what I've been through these past fourteen years. It's been so hard not telling anyone about it or not having Rockwell to confide in. He would have known what to do."

Now he was just rambling and making noise.

Andi pulled herself away from the viewing window with such a sense of almost mourning. Something she had lived with for so long was now gone. The unknown was gone. These past several minutes opened up many more questions relating to the people and activities of fourteen years ago, but with relief. Her big questions were answered!

Andi acknowledged Officer Hayden's presence with thanks and respect. They opened the door to their room and parted ways.

Andi went in search of Gayle. She and Chief Levi were alone in the interrogation room. Kevin had been led away by an unseen officer.

Levi looked at Andi and said, "That's a lot more than I thought we'd get, but I bet you two girls from Grafton figure there's a lot more to get. Oh, by the way, I already checked, so with the charges brought against Keven, he can be extradited to Massachusetts to face a judge."

"Thanks for that, Chief. But you are so right. There is much more to be looked into and learned here."

"Ladies, that is for tomorrow. As for today, I am done. Good night!" And the chief walked away with a little salute.

The Sabers

"How do you feel?" Gayle asked Andi.

"Relieved, stunned, numb. I was trying to put it into words, and I came up with…in mourning. A situation has died. Now we need to bury it! But knowing and being here, so close to his family, opens up more questions and feelings that I've never had to deal with, which may include Maddie. Do I dare go there?"

"Is that a real question? We can discuss it, or you can think on it for a while and maybe come up with a usable solution. Now let's get out of here," Gayle said, leading the way.

"Ya know what I want to do? Please don't think I'm sadistic."

Gayle waited.

"I want to meet Rachel. But more than that, I want all the Sabers and Mr. and Mrs. Schaffer to submit to a blood test. I need to know the source of the DNA matches. I can start there. With Kevin's arrest, I think a request would be denied, but a subpoena?" Andi looked at Gayle with hope in her eyes.

"We can talk to the chief in the morning. Let's go." Again, Gayle headed for the door.

Back in their motel room, Andi called home, needing to talk with Maddie, the stable beautiful little girl she left at home who was always happy to hear from her mother. Just hearing Maddie's voice brought home to her, the safe and comfortable place she made for the two of them. Next, Andi was excited to talk to Lynn and fill her in on the arrest of Kevin. In relaying the afternoon's interrogation and Kevin's breakdown toward and including his confession, he never verbally said the words *rape*, *assault*, and *sex*. He just accepted his arrest on the grounds of those words and actions.

"Now we have the arduous task of getting to the bottom of the fire and Rockwell's, as well as Kevin's, part in that. With Rockwell not being here to question, I don't believe we're ever going to get to the real truth of that incident. I'm also trying to find a DNA link in this mess! But give us a couple more days and we'll be home by the weekend."

Lynn was just happy to hear from Andi and hear the arrest news. It had been such a long and horrible road Andi had traveled. Now maybe she could live and love.

That had always been Lynn's wish for her best friend.

It wasn't until late afternoon the next day that Kevin was arraigned before the judge magistrate. At the same time, Chief Levi's subpoena of the Sabers and the Schaffers to be subjected to blood and saliva tests for DNA purposes, was granted. The judge had before him the micro-facts of 17 Speer Street, Grafton, Massachusetts, on April 12, 1964, and the autopsy report of number 8 from that scene. The judge was more than willing to approve that request. With his deepest regrets expressed toward Andrea Chambers for all the events that occurred, he also asked for a three notice when Kevin was extradited back to Massachusetts. With that, court was dismissed.

Before turning around in court, Chief Levi told Andi and Gayle that he and his staff had had a very busy morning pulling together the documents needed for the three finds that were just granted, but with a broad smile. He was happy to do it!

Without thinking, Andi hugged the chief and thanked him from the bottom of her heart.

Now when Andi turned to leave the courtroom, she noticed, for the first time, many people...familiar people. Mr. and Mrs. Schaffer were present as well as Mrs. Saber. And by the looks of it, her children too. Without a doubt, Andi had eyes on Rachel. Rachel had eyes on Andi.

Gayle was speechless. She looked at the two women who were mirror images of each other. Kevin's words came back to her. They more than looked alike!

Rhonda approached Andi very cautiously with an outstretched arm and hand in friendship. "May I buy you a drink or just coffee? Can we just sit and talk for a while?"

Andi shook her hand gratefully but answered cautiously, "With everything that has just happened, I'd love to talk with you, but we"—she looked at Gayle—"are still in the gathering information mode. We'd still be asking you a lot of questions."

Rachel stepped forward and said, "I'm coming along too. Mom said she met my double, so if we can ask you questions too, this could be a two-drink meeting. Let's make it dinner!"

Gayle accepted graciously and said, "Lead the way."

Once outside, Gayle and Andi followed Rhonda and Rachel to an American food restaurant featuring family-style service. Gayle said, "I guess the locals know the best places."

They were seated in a comfortable leather king's style chair at a round table for four. Drinks were ordered, and breads and crackers and flavored butters and cheese spreads were delivered, along with menus printed on wine bottles. It was a short menu featuring beef, chicken, pork, or Italian, all served family style. It was all-you-can-eat!

Simple…make it Italian. Everyone agreed.

For the first time in a long time, Andi felt totally comfortable and at ease. The past few days were exhausting and stressful. Sitting here with Rockwell's mother and his sister, who could pass as her own twin, should have made her nervous and self-conscious, but it didn't.

Gayle just looked at Andi, noticed the relaxed posture and ease of conversation, and was annoyed at herself for wanting to jump in with questions and take out a steno pad. She thought, *Just one.* "Rachel, how old are you?"

Rachel said, "So we are going to do this now…great. I'm thirty-two."

Andi said, "So am I…born in 1946."

Rachel countered with "Me too."

Rhonda reached out and touched both girls' hands. "I can't wait to get the DNA research done." Then she ordered another round of drinks.

"That was a great meal. The company wasn't so bad either. Rhonda and Rachel are nice people. They were a little on guard, but I guess so were we. I'm glad the meal meeting went the way it did," Gayle said while taking off her shoes and sitting on her bed back at their motel.

Andi giggled a little and said, "Whenever I have a good restaurant meal, I think of David in Arizona. I hope someday we can meet again."

Memories

The next day, Andi was back at 5 Lost Road, sitting with Rhonda in her big kitchen with Rachel and a few of her other kids sitting there just to get a look at her. The déjà vu feeling hit her again. She enjoyed the comfort of the camaraderie in the kitchen of the siblings. What would her life have been like…if…if…if…

Rhonda started with "I'm really glad you consented to come here today." She got up and lifted a top of a window seat, took out a big photo album, and brought it to the table. She immediately turned to a picture of someone who looked a lot like Andi's older brother, Aaron. Andi studied that picture, his hairline, the shape of his nose, his slight smile like he didn't want to get caught smiling. The glint in his eyes…

"That was the last picture I took of Rockwell."

"Ya know, truth be known, Rockwell was mom's favorite," Rachel added to the conversation.

"Absence makes the heart grow stronger, that's all," Rhonda quickly added.

Andi confided that he looked very much like her older brother and asked permission to look at the other pictures in the album.

While Rhonda got up for the coffee pot, Andi turned page after page of pictures that took her back to her childhood. By now, only

Rachel remained seated at the table with her and her mom. The other kids went on their merry way. Andi looked closer at a number of the pictures and thought she saw her own little brothers or sisters. The twins could have been Alley and Alex. There weren't many pictures of Rhonda with her children.

"It's because I was behind the camera. I took all of these pictures," she spoke up.

"Dad was home so little. Plus, he was very camera shy, so I bet there aren't any pictures of him either," Rachel added.

"Let me tell you, I've squandered the only picture of him I have in my own personal space. I'll be only a minute." And with that, Rhonda left the kitchen.

Rachel was all a tither, knowing her mom had a picture of her dad. She'd never seen it! "Let me see." She was on her feet when her mom came back to the table.

"Oh, Mom, that's a really good one. Ya know, Russell and Riley are the two that look very much like Dad."

Andi waited a minute and let Rachel enjoy seeing the picture. Then she asked if she could see it.

A very dark feeling came over Andi as she was looking at the man's picture. That strange but powerful feeling you got in the pit of your stomach when you knew that something was about to happen or that something wasn't right overtook Andi's whole being. *This can't be*, she thought in disbelief.

In a whisper, the words came out. "That's *my* dad!"

"Oh, so you had a good-looking father too," said Rhonda.

Andi just stared at the two women sitting looking back at her.

"I've only been in town for two days, but in that time, so much has happened. Once I met you, I knew we could possibility be friends.

220

You have a great family, and you are friendly and easy to talk to, but now I need to get down to brass tacks! I can tell that Rockwell holds a special place in your heart, and Kevin loved him very much as well. But look at the mess Kevin is in. I bet you didn't know…" Andrea looked around the table at the mother and daughter and didn't know if she could finish.

Rachel jumped in with "We are so sorry for what Kevin did to you. That's a side of Kevin we didn't know existed. We know he drinks a little too much sometimes, but we also thought he knew right from wrong. His poor mom and dad are besides themselves and are going to need help to get through this!"

Andi stood up like she was going to leave, but Rhonda's pleading look and soft touch on Andi's arm changed Andi's mind.

"I bet we didn't know a lot of things when it comes to Rockwell and Kevin's activities. Once they went off to college, they grew in a different direction. They both became men. Little boys grow up and leave home." Rhonda's heart was breaking, and Andi hadn't even told her the worst part yet.

Andi took her hand and said, "I'm glad Rockwell is not here now, because you'd be in the same boat as the Schaffers. Rockwell would be going to jail for arson and negligent homicide. He lit the fire at my folks' house and somehow couldn't escape himself. I'm sorry he died a horrible death, I really am, but so did my entire family! No one deserves to die like that."

The three of them sitting at the table had crocodile tears and broken hearts. For the moment, the worst was over!

"Kevin holds the key to so many secrets he and Rockwell shared," Andi ventured on. "Do you know anything about the pictures that were in Rockwell's position? It seems that pictures are the catalyst to many of the queries happening around here. That picture of your husband! Kevin said there was a picture of me. He said it looked a lot like Rachel! Rockwell had a bag of pictures that he shared with Kevin. We, the police, are trying to find that bag of pictures. Once we do, it will probably produce more questions, but that's how we get to the bottom of things.

"Sometimes the answers are not very kind and hurt a lot of lives. I don't think I can hurt anymore. I know I can be extremely surprised, but those surprises don't hurt me anymore. Life is full of surprises."

Just then, a young man holding a baby and two more kids at his feet came running in. The young woman took the baby, said, "Hi, Mom," kissed Rhonda's cheek, and sat.

Rhonda was delighted to introduce Russell and his wife, Cora, and she named Bruce, Anthony, and Anne-Marie, as the two oldest went in search of other people.

Andi held out her hand in greeting but was speechless by Russell's looks. Finding her tongue, she looked at Rachel and said, "You are right. He looks a lot like Dad...your dad."

Russell's handshake was firm but cautious. "So you're the woman who looks just like our Rachel...how, wow!"

Pictures

"Glad you're here, Russell. We were just talking about and looking at pictures. Look at this one." Rachel handed over the picture of their dad.

"I remember this...the background." Russell sat down and looked at his mother. "May I please have a cup of coffee? It's five o'clock somewhere. Put some whiskey in it."

"Capital idea," Rachel agreed. With drinks taken care of, Russell asked where the rest of the pictures were.

"What pictures?" Rhonda asked in total bewilderment. This conversation was getting weird.

Russel countered, "That picture is one either Rockwell or I took when we were on that marvelous vacation with Dad way back when. We were standing on the dock, waiting to board the ferry to the Statue of Liberty, and we took turns standing with Dad to take pictures and took one of him alone...this picture. Where did you find it?"

Rhonda's skin tone went from pink and happy to pale and nervous. "I do remember that vacation he took you boys on. It was a strange thing for him to do. He wasn't the daddy type, but the three of you went off so happy and returned even happier. How did you take pictures?"

"Don't you remember? Rockwell and I told you about it. Just out of town, Dad stopped at Harry's Handy Mart and let us buy all sorts of things. Both Rockwell and I bought those Instamatic 25 exposure cameras, and we filled them at all the stops we made." Russell held the picture and looked at it again and finished, "It's a great day to think back about Dad being that happy and fun…because he was. I wish Rockwell were here to remember with me! So again…where did this picture come from?" Russell's tone was dreamy and hopeful.

"Truth? I got it sent to me personally, in the mail, about a week after your vacation." Rhonda's voice sounded questioning. "Okay, the return address on the mailer was New York. The picture was taken in New York. I questioned it but dismissed my misgivings because I was happy to have the picture."

"So this is the only picture we have of our trip with Dad? What happened to all the pictures Rockwell and I took? Dad promised to send in the mailer and pay for processing. That was good enough for me. Total brain fart on remembering to ask him about them the next time he came home."

"So you never thought about it again and never saw the pictures the two of you took?" Andi questioned Russell one more time.

"Nope, never, till now. Just this one!"

"I wonder if those are the pictures that Kevin has. The ones he got from Rockwell that are in the bag," Andi wondered out loud.

Russell followed up with "If you find the bag of pictures, I can tell if we took them that week. Rockwell will know too. Sorry, Mom…brain fart!"

"Can Kevin have visitors? I'll go and ask him where the pictures are. I'm not a cop. He might talk to me," Russell volunteered.

Everyone at the table volunteered to drive him.

Russell

"That was the day Rockwell told me about the chock-a-mammy idea. He had to go to Grafton and get back at her mother!"

"Slow down," Russell said to Kevin. "What day are you talking about?"

"Okay…the day Rockwell found the pictures. He saw your mom's bedroom door open, so he went in. Your dad's chest on the floor was open. You know Rockwell, the biggest snoop that ever lived. Well, he went through it and found the pictures in a manila envelope. He returned the manila envelope, like it was never seen, dumped the pictures in a lunch bag, and came running over to my house. He was so angry with your dad. Kept saying, 'Mom can never know. Mom can never know.' That's all he would say. Except you've got to keep this secret! But I didn't know what the secret was…not then!"

Andi was in a viewing room with Gayle and Chief Levi while Russell had his visit with Kevin.

Levi said, "Now we're getting somewhere. Those pictures could be the key to this whole mess."

Looking at the two men behind the glass wall, Levi continued, "Keep him talking, Russell. So far so good."

"You said not then, so when did you know the secret?" Russell was still coaxing.

"On the way to Grafton, we stopped for a burger, and Rockwell confided in me. The lady in the picture, he said, was the pretty girl's mom, and your dad was banging her. The thought of that hurt him so bad and made him so angry. He said it was payback time. I get the girl, and he'd go after the mom. He never did tell me his exact intentions. He just said to meet him in the orchard at three a.m., and we'd get out of town. If that didn't work, we'd see each other back at the apartment on Wednesday." Kevin finished, hung his head, and cried. "Russell, I am so tired. I've been running those words in my head for fourteen years."

Andi sat in shock at Kevin's words. "There is no way," she said. "*No* way in hell! Not my mom!"

Gayle approached Andi and hugged her. "I know, honey. We'll get to the bottom of this. We need those pictures."

"Kevin, there is a lot hanging on those pictures. Can I get to them?"

"Sure, easy. In a leather zip bag under the spare tire in the trunk of my car. I look at them now and then. It brings Rockwell back, even though he's a little kid in them."

The threesome in the viewing room were out the door so fast. The chief radioed to the garage to have Kevin's car unlocked. It was still in the back impound lot. They reached it just as it was being unlocked. They popped the trunk, lifted the spare, and saw the leather pouch.

Back in the building with Russell as witness, they spread the pictures on a table and feasted their eyes!

"Hey, Russell, you and Rockwell were pretty cute kids," Gayle said to break the tension which was hovering over the room.

Andi just cried openly as she touched pictures of her father at the beach, at a cookout, standing with Rockwell. She was wrong. She could still hurt. These secrets were killing her!

Chief Levi handled three pictures, double exposures each showing what looked like a handwritten note on a TV screen or taped to a TV screen.

"This is a strange thing to take a picture of. Hey, Russell, put your thinking cap on. Do you remember these? Each a double exposure of something in the room, picking up a picture of a note taped to the TV."

"STEPPED OUT FOR A DRINK. BE BACK SOON."

Russell looked at the pictures, and his face crinkled in confusion. "Nope, don't remember these at all. It looks like the TVs that were in our motel rooms, sure. That's Rockwell's baseball cap on the tabletop. Never saw that note."

Russell, holding two pictures in his hands, leaned back in his seat and softly giggled. "You really had to be there to appreciate this, but see this woman." He was pointing to a well-endowed strawberry blond in the background wearing a skimpy top. "She butt patted me, kissed me on the cheek, handed me a beer, winked, and told me and this other guy to get lost! Rockwell did good getting picture!"

Gayle's dirty mind or suspicious mind was in overdrive. *His dad posts a note in the room in case the boys wake up. He goes just a few doors down and meets with another woman, maybe that strawberry blond, but three notes? Wow!*

"Russell, I'm really going to tax your memory on this. Can you start with your dad picking you guys up and tell me each stop and

227

each place you stayed? Can you put these pictures in order by those stops?" Gayle had a hunch that many miles apart, there would be familiar faces popping up. She needed to see if that hunch played out or if she was grasping at straws.

Russell started with stopping at the store to buy clothes. That's when they bought the cameras. He remembered the first time Cora (now his wife) was in his basement room. She made him get rid of the blond bombshell picture he posted on his ceiling. He got it that day.

"Then fishing, then supper at all-night diner…great! Lake Winnipesaukee, cleanest water I ever saw. Stopped at a Cracker Barrel on the way to Hampton Beach. Ocean, water slides, skating, cookouts, beer, that woman. Started for some old village in Massachusetts, but it was closed. Went to a movie, went to an apple orchard, ate hot dogs at a neat shack on the side of the road."

Andi grabbed two of the pictures Russell just put on the table and started crying her eyes out. "That's my mom! That's me and Mom."

Russell stopped for a minute, went to Andi, and hugged her. "Yup, you look just like Rachel. Your mom's pretty too. Russell continued, "We went to New York City, stayed at a hotel…thirty-first floor. Went to the Statute of Liberty. Came home. Dad said we ate our way north then south again! With memories as great as that, how do things go so terribly wrong!"

Gayle was labeling the stops as Russell talked. All this time, Russell was putting pictures near the printing.

"Russell, sorry to burst your bubble, but I now see what I think Rockwell saw or guessed at when he studied these pictures. The note clearly indicates he left you guys alone in the room, and he was covering his ass! My guess, these double exposure pictures were not meant to be taken. It caught the note on the TV. Your dad never gave you guys the pictures, and Rockwell guessed the note was to be with a woman. Go to your New York pictures…on the dock. Look at the woman with the colorful scarf on her head. Look at her face. Compare with the beer lady at the cookout. One note in Hampton Beach, one note in New York."

"We stayed two nights at Hampton Beach," Russell said with a scowl.

"I'd need to examine the actual note, but I bet he used the same one every time."

Andi left the room with a few of the pictures. She went downstairs to the holding cells to find Kevin.

"Kevin, this picture." Andi held it up for Kevin to look at.

"Yeah, it's you."

"The woman in the driver's seat, ever see her before?"

"Yeah, a picture at a cookout…great boobs! You look like your mother."

"Did Rockwell tell you this was my mother?"

"No, but you were with her at that house in Grafton. You got out of her car at your house, right?"

"Did Rockwell tell you these were the same women?"

"He didn't have to. I have eyes."

Andi held both pictures up for him to look at. "Yeah, that's the woman."

Andi went back upstairs and reported what she just learned.

"Kevin identified the women in both of these pictures as the same woman."

Gayle took the pictures from Andi. She looked at them and gave them to Levi.

Levi turned to Russell and said, "Hey, are these the same woman?"

Out loud, he was rambling, "About the same body shape, about the same height, about the same color hair." He took out his wallet and passed around a picture of his mom holding his oldest son… same body shape, about the same height, about the same color hair. He smirked. A little redder and wilder, but…no…she was a third!

Russell wandered back over to his chair, still studying the pictures. He sat still for a long time. Andi recognized the look of anguish when she looked over at Russell slouched a bit in the chair, eyes closed, lips moving ever so slowly, legs stretched out straight but jumping every now and then, and hands totally fisted with the pictures laying in his lap.

He never opened his eyes when Andi went to him. She announced she was there before touching his left forearm when she sat next to him.

"I've had more than fourteen years to prepare for these past few days. For the first time in all those years, I know who my rapist is. I've learned more about the madman who took my family from me. I'm glad facts are coming into view. I'm sorry you didn't have the time to prepare for these hard heartbreaking facts. You and your entire family are kind and caring people. You've demonstrated that to me. I needed that to realize that Rockwell just snapped when he saw the real man behind his dad and caught him red-handed in lies and behavior he couldn't understand or tolerate. I can now bury the monster I made Rockwell out to be for my own sense of relief and enjoy my daughter and the rest of my life."

"These facts…are we on the same page? Really?" Russell opened his eyes, sat up a bit straighter, pulled his legs in, put the pictures on the table next to him, and took Andi's hands in his.

"Do you even know your last name? Do I? How did he get away with being Reginald Sabers and Aspen Chambers for all these years? Who else was he? Who was he really? A captain in the Army? A captain in the Navy? He spent four days a month with my mom. How much time did he spend with yours? Who helped him with his life of deceit? Where did his money come from? Was your dad really buried with the rest of your family? Your dad was a bigamist. I'm your half brother. Our brother killed our father. One of our best friends is your daughter's father. Your daughter is my niece. My brother killed his own flesh and blood all living in Grafton and died because of it. Dad broke every rule in the book, and you know who is left to live with it? *My mom!*"

Epilogue

It's really odd what can trigger the memories, but it happened again as it had so many times over the years. Maybe it was the warmth of the wonderful spring day or the way the apple blossoms filled the air with their fragrance. Maybe this time, it was just that Andrea needed the youthful feelings which were associated with the memories and the could have beens.

Many years ago, the husband of Andrea's best friend planted six apple trees along her back property line. Today, she was sitting in the gazebo in her backyard, enjoying their blossoms and fragrance, waiting for her daughter, Maddie, and her husband, Ethan, to arrive for Sunday dinner. It was a special day. It was Mother's Day. Therefore, Maddie's three beautiful children would be arriving with their children as well. Since she retired, she lived for these days. She remembered long ago when dinner for this many family members was no big deal!

While she waited, she spent the morning reading the paper, and always the obituaries. So many of her old friends had passed on.

Worcester Sunday Telegram, May 9, 2010
Obituaries p. 9
Legal Notices: Posted by Law

Andi always wondered about these people and their lives.

By law, it was posted that Vincent Octavio Clear, alias Reginald Sabers, alias Aspen Chambers, alias Keith Rogers, was laid to rest in an unmarked plot in Grafton, Massachusetts, as per his dying request. The only person in attendance was his lawful wife of sixty-one years, Crystal Clear.

About the Author

Diane Brooks is the oldest of seven children. She was brought up in a home full of love and noise and one bathroom! Her dad is nothing like the one she'd written about but rather a wise ninety-four-year-old who still swaps books with her and tends a large vegetable garden. This year, 2021, she is to become a *memere* ("grammy" in French) for the first time in November while celebrating her fiftieth wedding anniversary to the love of her life. Someday, her grandchild will know that she is of the 1960s generation, who wore bell-bottom pants, never wore a seat belt, had wild long hair, smoked cigarettes in the girls' room in high school, and enjoyed Woodstock.

She has quit smoking, always wears a seat belt, her hair has gone quite gray but is still wild and crazy, and she still believes they had the best music!

She's having a hard time retiring, so writing is keeping her company and busy.

CPSIA information can be obtained
at www.ICGtesting.com
Printed in the USA
BVHW082059150222
629079BV00003BA/173

9 781662 463310